Another Life

by
Andrew Foote

Chapter One.

From which ever direction you approach Birmingham, you have go up hill. Not by much but it made a serious difference temperature-wise and I was bloody cold!

I had taken myself out of school that lunchtime. My life had become like so much shit and then some, but whilst it seemed like a good idea then, it definitely didn't right now, not that I wasn't relieved to get away from home, I was, but like most kids, I'd done what I had done on a whim without thinking strategy.

I had spent the afternoon wandering the streets not really bothered that I was still in school uniform, actually, as it turned out, it had done me a favour as I was quizzed by a police officer asking why I was out of school.

An easy question to lie to as I told him I had a dental appointment.

Well, he seemed satisfied enough.

As dusk fell and the temperature dropped, I realised that I had to find some place to sleep and stay out of sight. I had watched programs on TV that showed men dossing in alleyways with only a cardboard box for shelter, so I went on the lookout for some-where / something suitable.

I got chased away from the busy places, something about being jail bait, a problem waiting to happen, and so I ventured deeper into the shit that is inner city England, places occupied by rats and vermin like the rear entrances of iffy fast-food outlets and mas-sage parlours, but then I noticed a hole in a wall, not that big but big enough for me to get through, and once I'd wriggled my way inside, I lit a match hoping that it was enclosed, not open to the elements.

In the event, the roof was intact, it was dry, and bonus! I found a large cardboard box partially filled with expanded polystyrene chips, so peeling off the outer layers of my clothing, I settled down for the night.

*****

"Hey you? What you at? That's my pissing box you're in so get the fuck out!"

I scrubbed at my eyes only to see a weak torch aimed at me but then whoever was holding it spoke again.

"Fuck me! You're a kid!"

"Yes, well, I'm sorry, but I was knackered and needed somewhere to be. I didn't mean to trespass, honestly. I'll go and find somewhere else."

"What? At this time of night? Get real, sunshine, the Bill will be all over you in seconds flat. You look like shit, are you okay?"

"Em……..I'm not sure to be honest. Who are you anyway?"

"My place so I do the questions but my name, for what it's worth is Callum……..just Callum, right? Yours is?"

"Edward. Edward Ander…….."

"Edward's enough. The least we know about each other the better. When was the last time you ate?"

"Breakfast, I had a couple of slices of toast."

"Jesus, Edward? You thinking of living on the streets on an empty stomach? Dumb move, dumb move! Got to keep up your energy levels up, or sure as shit, the cold will get to you, so bugger off and get fed. Ronny's place just down the road is alright, and before you leave there, take a piss, a crap if you need one 'cos I don't need you messing up this place...... I have to live here, you as well if you behave."

"I'm okay. I'm not hungry. Thanks anyway."

"You mean you're skint more like. Here's a fiver, go and fill yourself up and you can pay me back some other time. While you're gone, I'll see if I can find something half decent for you to sleep in. Now fuck off!"

*****

I found Ronny's, not difficult to clock what with the number of black cabs outside and a flashing neon sign saying 'Open 24 Hours'.

I stepped inside turning heads as I made my way to the counter.

"Well, son? What can I do for you then?"

"Em...... I'm starved. What's good?"

"All my food's good. Who sent you?"

"Sent me?"

"Yeah, sent you! This here's whore town, we don't get many chickens round here so......?"

"I don't understand. Chickens?"

"Yeah, well, never mind. Was it Callum?"

"Yes...... do you know him?"

"Nah, never heard of him...... *of course I know him!!*"

"Sorry. Anyhow he said you served decent food."

"You got money?"

"Um...... only what he lent me."

"Well, well! He *has* taken a shine to you! I've got the remains of today's roast, good enough for you?"

"How much is it? He only gave me five quid?"

"A mate of Callum's is a mate of mine, so no charge, eat and enjoy."

"Are you sure?"

"No, I'm not bloody sure, so eat it before I change my mind."

He turned away, shaking his head before disappearing behind a bead curtain, muttering, "There better be a God up there...... fucking rent boys eating me out of house and home......"

*****

The meal was pretty good actually, and I said as much.

"Pleased you think so. The toilet's round the back, just mind the rats, okay? I'll get some coffee's to take back with you, and by the way...... take it steady out there. Not everyone is as nice as me so keep your wits about you."

*****

I found Callum kneeling beside a second cardboard box busy breaking up some polystyrene.

"Found it then? Not all bad grub and Ronny's an okay bloke."

"Yes, he seemed friendly enough, and by the way. Here's your fiver. He didn't let me pay, gave us some coffee as well."

"Remind me to thank him. Got you your own box so take care of it 'cos they're like rocking horse shit round here, and keep the dosh. Always good to have summat in your pocket. When we go out tomorrow, keep your eyes open for old newspapers...... good insulation against the cold."

He stood up and obviously pleased with his work, gestured to me to climb in.

Hey, it was comfortable and surprisingly warm.

"Thanks Callum, that was very nice of you."

"Yeah, I'm a nice person!"

"Ronny said as much as well."

"Well, he would, being my business manager an' all."

"Can I ask you something?"

"Look Edward. I'm bushed, so let's talk in the morning, huh? Try and get some sleep, but before you do, are you, like, alright? It's pretty obvious that you're new to all this and I just wondered......?"

"Last night I slept in a comfy bed and in a centrally heated house...... tonight? Okay, I'm homesick, but I'm happy enough because life was crap there. Warm and comfortable but all the time being used as a punch bag and worse...... much worse, versus being away from all that abuse, then yeah, I'm okay."

"Good enough. Get some shut-eye, we've all day tomorrow to talk. Nite."

*****

I woke late to the noise of traffic and the bin men going about their business. I glanced at my watch...... nine fifteen and late for school.

That thought made me laugh. What sodding school?

Callum turned over and for the first time I could see his face sort of clearly. He wasn't as old as I'd first thought, probably not that much older than me. Jet black hair which immediately made me assume he was of Indian, decent but as he opened his eyes, this definitely wasn't the case as his eyes had the almond shape I'd always associated with Chinese or at least those of oriental persuasion.

He was good-looking…… very attractive actually. He had nice lips, nice long eyelashes and…… I liked what I saw.

"Hey Edward? What's the time?"

"Almost half nine. Did you get a good night's sleep?"

"No, it was rubbish. Some fucking kid kept me awake most of the night with his snoring!"

"Oh God? I'm sorry?"

"Just kidding you! I slept for England, and so far as I'm aware, you don't snore, okay? Are you hungry?"

"Actually I am a bit. Do you go to Ronny's?"

"Fucking-hell no! First rule of living on the streets is that you only move around at times outside of school hours. Before nine in the morning, between twelve and one-thirty then after three-thirty in the afternoon. Work outside of those hours and you run the risk of being lifted by the cops or the truancy people, so no, we eat in-house so to speak."

"I almost got fingered yesterday but I was in my school uniform and told him I had a dentist appointment. Lucky me I guess!"

"Got to get them dry cleaned. Those might prove to be a massive asset. Anyhow, breakfast. Walk this way."

Callum took me through into a sort of passageway which stank of diesel, then through a door which opened onto a concreted area which backed on to a canal.

"Your own garden terrace, complete with a water vista, a barbeque breakfast and then we can talk. Behind that tarpaulin you'll find a fridge. Give me some bacon, sausages and eggs and I'll cook while you butter some bread. You'll find a couple of plates in the shed but make sure they're clean, knives and forks as well."

*****

A barbequed breakfast, definitely a first for me and not all bad either. We ate in silence, and then once we'd finished, Callum put the plates and cutlery into a carrier bag.

"Want some coffee?"

"Yes, thank you. Coffee would be good."

"You haven't tasted it yet. I've got no sugar and the milk's gone off, so I hope you take it black and bitter...... one other thing, it's not decaf."

"Whatever's fine."

We sat around watching the boats and drinking coffee by the bucket full. Callum produced a tobacco tin and offered me a roll-up before lighting one for himself.

"I don't smoke thanks."

"Please yourself.

Okay then. Tell me about Edward."

"What do you want to know?"

"Walk me through your life. I need to understand why a nice, polite and educated kid ends up dossing on the streets."

"Alright. I'm nudging sixteen years old and up until yesterday I lived with my mother and her man friend in Solihull."

"Posh kid then?"

"We used to be, that is until my father took it upon himself to leave. Do you want me to carry on?"

"Yeah. Do that."

"Okay. I went to Hatton Grammar School as a day pupil. I was lucky as I got a scholarship so they didn't have to pay any fees, but you're not interested in that."

"No, not really."

"Everything was fine until my father left us. I still don't fully understand why he did what he did, my mother won't talk about it. He still pays the mortgage on the house and provides for my mother and me, but these days she spends most of it on drink and drugs. I'm telling you, she's a real mess. Anyway. Next she finds herself a bloke, a serious head-case. I mean, who on earth drinks vodka for breakfast? Well he does. The thing is, from there on in they both just slide into a drunken mess and I've even seen my mother attempting to shoot up but she's so pissed, she can't see what she's doing so she takes it out on me, screaming and shouting, throwing furniture at me which in turn causes her bloke to get all worked up and joins in the fray.Here. Take a look at this."

I lifted my shirt.

"Shit, Edward? They did that to you?"

"Yeah, and this isn't the worst it's been either."

"But didn't your school pick up on it? I mean, didn't you have to get changed for sports, shower or whatever?"

"Yes, but I got pretty good at hiding it and skipping showers was easy enough."

"You could've gone to Social Services? Why didn't you do that?"

"Difficult to explain. I thought that they might straighten themselves out. Stupid really 'cos that was never going to happen, and also, blood's thicker than water. I loved my mum, and if I had reported stuff then I'd be taken into care and never see her again."

"Yeah maybe. What happened next?"

"The night before last, I got back from school only to find both of them totally out of it. I mean, like they were unconscious, so my immediate instinct was to leave them to it, but when I went up to my room, the entire contents, and I do mean *EVERYTHING,* had been trashed. My laptop, my games consul, my bed, most of my clothes had been shredded, my bank book was missing, I mean, the list goes on. All the windows had been smashed, the curtains ripped. My fucking room looked worse than where we slept last night!"

"So that's when you upped and left?"

"No, not straight away. I still had my phone so I called the police and ambulance, *then I legged it."*

"Where did you stay that night?"

"I hid in the shed! Once the police had left and my mother and her bloke carted off to hospital, I went back inside, but then the next morning I packed what I could into my backpack and did a runner. The rest you know."

"I never saw a backpack? Did you lose it?"

"No. I took the train from Solihull to Moor Street Station where I rented a storage locker. It's still there."

"What's in it?"

"What clothes I could find that were still in one piece, a toilet bag, my passport and MP3, and what cash I could lay my hands on which didn't amount to much.

Oh, yeah. I found my bank book, but that arsehole had withdrawn everything, presumably to fund his addiction."

"Okay then. Here's what we do. We go and retrieve your backpack at lunchtime. How much time did you pay on the locker?"

"Five days."

"Okay, so that means you should be able to get a refund for four of them which will give you another twenty quid in your pocket, plus you can get out of that uniform so we can get it cleaned. Then I reckon you should get yourself looked at. You got pretty badly worked over, so it's better to ere on the side of caution."

"I can't just go wandering into a hospital or to a doctor's surgery?"

"No need. I'll take you to see the dodgy doc. He'll sort you out."

"The what doc?"

"Dodgy as in iffy. He got himself struck off after he served time for tinkering around with little boys. He knows what he's at, so you've nothing to worry about."

"Haven't I? You're telling me he's a paedophile, yet I've nothing to be worried about?"

"Nah! I'll tell him I'll give him a freebee if he keeps his hands off you. That should do the trick!"

"*Freebee??* You mean like you're......"

"Yeah, I'm on the rent. Everybody had to earn a crust."

"I hope you don't expect me to......"

"Calm down, Edward. It's cool. I don't expect anything from you!"

"Thanks, but I can't expect you to keep feeding me for nothing."

"You're right there, I've no idea what, but we'll find something to occupy your time"

"So, what's your story then?"

"You wanna know about me? Yeah, well, why not. There's not much to tell really but here goes.

My parents came to England when I was about two, I think. They later told me that actually, I wasn't their son, and looking back, they were too old to have been, but no matter. They originally came from Vietnam...... both of us are too young to remember the Vietnam war, but it split the country in two and lots of people had to leave or face all sorts of shit, and my folks were amongst them, Vietnamese boat people they called them, but anyway, they fled the country and settled in Korea, which was okay but the Commies took over the north, which is where they were, and they got kicked over the border into the south. The problem was that they weren't welcome there either, so to escape deportation, they hid, running from village to village, sometimes getting some work, sometimes not...... most of the time not.

They did eventually find a place that accepted them, and this is where I come into the picture. A farming accident happened and, so I'm told, killed both my natural parents, so I was taken in by the people who raised me, those I call my parents. Then came the redevelopment of the area, factories and so on, and with them came more police. My parents spoke Korean but with a different dialect so they were sussed out pretty quick. They had little choice but to do another runner taking me with them.

They ended up in Taipei, then my father managed to pay some ship's Captain to give us passage to Europe, but the tub we had sailed in went aground off the Minkies. Rescuers came from mainland France and most were picked up, but not us. We were adrift on a life raft for forty-eight hours before an English fishing trawler spotted us and took us back to their home port. The Skipper of that trawler took pity on us and gave my father some money telling him to head for a big city where we could lose ourselves...... he chose Brum! Anyway, obviously they didn't hide very well because one night the immigration people came calling, they were arrested and later deported, and me?

I was much better at hiding!"

"Oh my God! That's awful? Not much of a story you say? For Christ's sake, Callum??"

"Yeah, but you've got to remember, most of this I don't remember. My earliest memories are of living in Birmingham."

"Where abouts?"

"Ha! Alum Rock...... the public toilet of all humanity, the Dignitas of the fucking world!

Fuck it, Edward? You think here's bad?

NOTE: Dignitas is a clinic in Switzerland that assists people to commit suicide.

Chapter Two.

Beings as it was gone twelve, we ambled through the streets as we made our way to Moor Street Station. Callum had warned me about looking nervous or holding the eyes of any cop we might see and just to make casual contact then carry on as if it was perfectly normal for us to be out doing whatever we were doing.

It worked, and we were never challenged.

We collected my bag, got a refund then made tracks for our hideaway before questions could be asked of us.

We managed to get back safely and sitting out by the canal, I emptied the contents of my backpack onto the concrete. There wasn't much. Three decent shirts, two pairs of jeans, socks and underwear, three tee shirts and two thick jumpers. I'd also packed into a separate carrier bag, a pile of books, some were school books, but mostly I'd loaded it down with my favourite fiction, and in between the pages I had hidden what cash I'd managed to find.

"So, how much do you have there?"

"I'm not sure. Fifty quid maybe?"

"Okay, so enough to keep you going for a few weeks then, so long as you stick with the essentials that is.

Do you read a lot?"

"Yeah I do. It used to spirit me away into fantasy land, you know, stop me thinking about my home life. Sad aren't I."

"No. Actually, I envy you."

"How come?"

"I can't read. I'm seriously dyslexic. Fuck it? I can't even understand numbers which is why Ronny takes care of my money. I told you he was my business manager, didn't I."

"That's bad Callum? Don't you bank your money?"

"Yeah, but when I get statements, they mean bugger-all to me. Ronny might even be ripping me off, I dunno, because I don't get what those statements mean."

"Would you like me to take a look at them?"

"Might be good. Ronny is always carping on about how it is that he sorts out everything for me. Would you mind?"

"No, I'd be happy to. After my father left, I used to manage our household finances, my mother was too pissed most of the time, but then 'he' came on the scene and he would hit me if I went so much as close to them."

"Good. Thanks. We'll get to his place for a meal tonight and I'll get them off him."

Callum fell silent for a moment then touched my arm.

"Could you do me one other favour, Edward?"

"Sure. I will if I can. Ask away."

"Could you like, read to me sometime? I know it sounds childish, but no one has read a story to me since my folks were deported."

"I can do that. It'd be nice actually. What sort of stuff do you like?"

"Anything. Like you said, it would be nice to escape from reality. What do you like?"

16

"Adventure mysteries mostly. I'm a massive Clive Cussler fan!"

"Sounds good. Could we start like right now?"

"Why not? You pick a book from the pile."

Callum spread the books around, then looking at the pictures on the flysheets, made his selection.

"This one. I like stories about the sea, ships and what have you. Is that okay?"

"Yes. Nice choice. It's a fave of mine too!"

Callum, rather than sporting his disinterested posture, actually looked excited. "I can't believe I'm so looking forward to something for once! Normally sleep is the only event in any given day that I actively look forward to."

"I just hope I'm up to the task then. Shall I begin?"

*****

"Chapter one.

'To a casual onlooker, the 'Oregon' appeared to be a disaster waiting to happen. Her rusted hull and superstructure, unloved and uncared for, her decks littered with the debris of long unfinished repairs, her windows, most of which were either severely damaged or completely missing, paid tribute to a vessel that should have been consigned to the breakers yard long since, but behind this façade, this theatre set put together in order to deter other ships from getting too close, lay a beast waiting to be set loose.

Beyond this, she was perhaps one of the finest and most technologically advanced ships afloat, bristling with weaponry and communications equipment, her propulsion systems, comprising of highly secret turbines that extracted water from the sea, then separating the oxygen, used the hydrogen to fuel the burners thus giving her an unlimited source of fuel that powered her to a frightening sixty-five knots, but for the time being, were hardly having to break sweat as she knifed through the water at a mere twenty.

Captain Ed Anderson stood on the bridge and took stock.

"When do we hit landfall Ben?"

"04.00 hrs then we should be in Lebanese territorial waters."

"Get Mac to list her to starboard by 15 degrees and send out a distress call. Given our manifest shows we're supposed to be carrying liquid Ammonium Peroxide, they'll never in a million years allow us a berth, so lots of smoke from the stacks please.

I'm going below to take a shower and get changed into my scruffs. Give me a shout when the pilot is on the way."'

*****

"Chapter fifteen.

You still awake?"

"Yeah but it's getting a bit chilly out here. Let's go inside and see if we can get the fire to light."

"I didn't notice a fireplace?"

"Come on, I'll show you."

Once inside, Callum pointed to a sheet of hardboard propped up against the wall.

"It's behind there. I keep it blocked off unless I light it 'cos it draws like hell sucking cold air in through the hole in the wall. I keep meaning to knock out more of the brickwork and fit some sort of door, but I'm useless when it comes to that sort of thing."

"Between us we should be able to do it? My father owned a building firm and sometimes I would help out, or should that read hindered!"

"No harm in trying. Let's see if it'll light then we can leave it to warm the place up a bit while we grab a bite to eat."

*****

"Well, that came as a surprise! I honestly thought Ronny might bitch about handing over all my banking stuff. Maybe he hasn't been creaming some off the top!"

"Do you want me to take a look at it now?"

"Nah. Do it in the morning, I'd much prefer you to carry on reading to me. That book's brilliant!

The Captain. Is his name really Ed whatever?"

I giggled! "Nope! That's my name. I sort of borrowed him so I could be part of the story, I suppose, be a part of the fantasy."

"I like that! Could you do the same with me? That would be so cool!"

"No probs but you never told me what your family name is."

"Lee. Callum Lee."

"Okay then. There's a character coming up in the next chapter. He's like the head of operations, sort of like a Commando, tough and fearless but fair and kind of caring.

Sound familiar?"

"No, should it?"

"Yeah, 'cos he's just like you. You're tough and fearless but also you're kind, maybe even gentle."

"Piss off!"

"Why? You've got to be tough if you've managed to survive up 'till now. You don't seem afraid of much, and you took me in instead of kicking me out into the street, which means you're kind."

"Or crazy. The jury's still out on that one. What about this gentle bit then?"

"I dunno. I just get the impression that if you were ever to fall in love, it'd be all consuming, tender and passionate. You'd treat your girlfriend like she was the most important person in the world and then some. In short? You'd be gentle and loving."

"Phff. There's one major flaw in that argument. I'm gay, or maybe you've forgotten."

"You never said you were gay, just that you were on the rent. Does that mean you enjoy what you do?"

"*Enjoy it?? I fucking hate it!!* Look, Ed...... can I call you Ed?"

"No. Call me Captain!"

"Fuck off! Look, I do what I do in order to survive. Get real, Ed? Imagine what it's like to have some pervy old bloke pawing at you, expecting you to blow him until he cums in your mouth? Some of them wanna fuck you, for Christ's sake! Enjoy it? In your dreams!"

"Oh yuck!"

"Yuck indeed. Some of them are sort of sad now I come to think about it, like there's this one guy who just wants me to do a striptease while he wanks himself. He's never so much as laid a finger on me, but he pays me fifty quid for the privilege. Some of them cream themselves before they get around to doing anything. Hey, I've got a cute bod, I know I have, so if they wanna pay me just for getting them off, then I'll do it."

"I don't get it. In one breath you tell me you're gay, but in the next you say you don't like what you do?"

"I'm not into men you idiot! Now, if I was to have a boy-friend? Yeah, that would be nice."

"I'll keep an eye open for one, shall I?"

"Oh, yeah! Who the hell is going to hitch up with a dosser like me? If I went to school, maybe mixed with kids my age then...... well, it might be different, but as things stand, the only kids I know are like me and none of them interest me.

Can we please change the subject? I've said too much already."

*****

'Callum Lee stealthily inched his way towards the silos that housed the nuclear warheads then waited for his planned diversion to kick in.

He had rigged a small explosive device to a drum of kerosene, the idea being that the ensuing blaze would ensure that all the guards and the personnel in the accommodation block would be too preoccupied fighting the fire to notice him.

Callum, a veteran SAS Major, was well versed in the use of explosives, but to remove the detonators from a nuclear bomb was something even he couldn't manage, leaving him just one option, break into the silo and blow it up.

That was the easy bit, it got more complicated when he thought about how he'd get back to the 'Oregon', but that could wait.

Whoompf!

'There goes five hundred gallons of Kerosene' he muttered. 'Just hope the body of that guard is enough to fool them into thinking my little surprise was just an unfortunate accident.'

"I like my character Ed! He's really cool!"

"I'm pleased. He's gay too, by the way."

"No shit! Really?"

"Well, not in the book he isn't, but I'll make him that way if you want?"

Callum looked at me intently. "Yeah, I reckon you could at that."

"What?"

"Turn a straight SAS Major gay. You've got the looks right enough."

"Should I take that as a compliment?"

"Maybe a back-handed one. I'm beat. Let's get some shut-eye."

*****

"Okay, so what do you want to do first, Bank statements or breakfast?"

"Em...... breakfast I reckon. What money's on my account is-n't going to alter but I must look after my sweet body or sure as shit, there won't be *any money* going in anytime soon."

"Look, Callum? I know how you make your money, but really, do you have to keep reminding me?"

"What's up, Ed? Don't tell me you've got religion already?"

"No, nothing remotely like that. I just don't like thinking of you doing stuff with men."

"Well, I do, so live with it."

"Fine! Just don't keep reminding me like you're proud of yourself or something." I yelled.

With that, I burst into tears and ran outside and sat by the canal.

It wasn't long before Callum came out and sitting beside me, put his arm around my shoulder.

"What triggered that, Edward? I mean, we've talked about it before, and yes, I know how you feel about it, for fuck's sake, I feel much the same way, but you never went off on one before?"

"I don't know. Maybe it's because I'm still in a bit of a mess about my Mum. I don't even know if she's alive. Last time I saw her, she was unconscious."

"Can't you find out?"

"How! March into the hospital and say, 'Hi. I'm Edward Anderson. I called the ambulance to my Mum two days ago, and I wondered, is she still breathing?'
Come on?"

"No. Well, perhaps not! Tell you what? Why not phone the hospital."

"Could do, but what if they ask who I am? They don't just go giving out that sort of information to anybody?"

"You lie to them, tell them you're her nephew."

"But what if the cops have put a trace on my phone. It's on contract."

"Use mine. It's pay-as-you-go. Problem sorted."

"Thanks. I might just do that."

"No, not 'might just' Ed. Bloody-well do it and now while I rustle up some food."

*****

"Hello. I'm enquiring about a Mrs Anderson. Do you know of her? She was admitted the night before last."

"Yes we do. She's on ward twenty. Would you like me to connect you?"

"Yes. Thank you."

I was put on hold for what seemed like an eternity then finally...... "Ward Twenty, Sister Anne speaking?"

"Oh, good morning Sister. My name is Donald Turner, I'm Mrs Anderson's nephew. Could you tell me how she is please?"

"Well, you must understand that as you're not her immediate family, I'm not permitted to say that much. All I can tell you that her condition is critical but stable."

"But she'll be okay?"

"She's out of intensive care. Does that help?"

"Yes, lots. Thanks Sister."

"You're welcome. Why not call again in a day of two. We might be able to update you."

"I'll do that! Thanks."

*****

"News?"

"Out of intensive care, critical but stable. More than that she wouldn't say."

"Well, if nothing else, you know she's alive at least. Eat up before it gets cold, then once you've finished, brew some coffee while I give the fire a kick. I've got a feeling the weather's on the turn."

"How do you know?"

"Easy. The wind is coming from the North East and with it clear skies. That can only mean it's going to get seriously cold, especially overnight. If we get cloud then it'll most likely snow, and that, Edward, we really don't need!"

"I don't understand? I rather like snow?"

"Yeah, well, I like looking at it, it even makes this shithouse look passably clean, but think about it for a moment. How do we get in and out of here?"

"Through the hole in the wall."

"Correct. So if it snows, then what? Footprints leading every Tom, Dick and Harry to our hidey-hole, that's what!"

"Oh shit. What happens then?"

"We try and get out through the yard next door. There's a gap in the fence just behind the fridge, but during the day, the yards in use so we have to be like ultra-careful we're not spotted."

"What about at night time. Isn't it locked?"

"Yes but I managed to figure out the combination! No worries on that score."

*****

Three nights on and Callum's weather forecast was proved correct. I've no idea just how cold it was but the fire made little or no difference to our room, so as his bank account was showing deposits to the tune of a tad over two grand, we went into town and bought a couple of sleeping bags, stole five bags of coal from next doors yard and settled into a long hibernation, only stepping outside for essentials and to cook breakfast.

"I wonder how the other kids are doing. Some of them little bastards live in worse places than this."

"How many others are there?"

"Last count? I dunno, twenty maybe? Some of them might've been sussed out, so it's hard to tell precise numbers."

"Maybe they're the lucky ones!"

"Yeah, maybe you're right. How would you feel if I went out on a sortie and got them to come here until the weather changes?"

"It's your place so……"

"*Our place!* What do you reckon?"

"Invite them. Yes, definitely invite them!"

"I was hoping you'd say that. Want to come along for the ride?"

"What, and leave a nice warm fire? Okay, I'm in."

"Good. Maybe you'll see just how lucky we are having this place."

*****

Callum wasn't wrong. How some of these poor kids managed to survive was a complete mystery to me, I'm pretty sure I'd be dead by now had I been one of them.

Most wanted to come with us but not all so I asked about this.

"Surely all of them would rather have a roof over their heads, so why are there a few who want to tough it out?"

"Pride, Ed. All of these kids are used to sorting stuff for themselves. They don't much like being beholding to other people, sort of goes against the grain. Stupid, but there you have it."

Some of the kids brought along their own boxes but a few didn't which begged another question from me.

"Those four over there didn't bring anything to sleep in. Given that boxes are in short supply, what do we do with them?"

"I'd thought about that as well, so what I thought we might do is lend them ours. We can line the floor with newspapers then sleep in front of the fire. We've got sleeping bags, remember?"

"Yes, but that only takes care of two of them."

"Nah. We get them to double up. They'll probably be warmer than us!"

That evening it was time to start on another book, but this time I had an audience of seventeen, eighteen if I included Callum.

Callum picked another 'Oregon' adventure as he liked his character! It was a blast and I read for over two hours, but then noticing some of the younger kids yawning, I knocked it on the head.

We lined the floor with as many old newspapers as we could lay our hands on, then stripping out of our outer layers of clothing, dived into our respective sleeping bags.

Bloody-hell it was cold! I tried to sleep but the newspaper idea wasn't having the desired effect, the cold was seeping through, chilling me to the bones.

I obviously wasn't alone.

"Are you awake, Ed?"

"Yes. I'm too fucking cold to sleep! I can't feel my feet, and the cold coming up from the floor is a killer."

"I've got the same problem. I hesitate to ask, but what if we were to share? We could use one bag to help insulate the floor, double up on the newspapers as will only need space for the one bag, and anyway, our combined body heat should do the trick. What do you think?"

"Works for me. Those kids seem to be alright, so yeah, let's do it."

We busied ourselves rearranging the newspapers and placing the spare sleeping bag on top of them, crawled into the second.

It was strange being so damned close to another human being, a nice strange though. It had the desired effect as we both began to stop shivering.

Callum let out a moan. "Not now? Please not now?"

"What's the matter?"

"I've gone and popped one."

"Like as in………"

"Yeah. I've got a hard-on."

"Why?"

"What do you mean, why! Cuddling up with a cute boy is why. I'm gay, you're cute to the point of…… cute and you ask why? May God preserve us Edward. Sometimes I worry about you!"

"Ignore it and try to get some sleep."

"If you pop one, can you ignore it? It's fucking impossible at our age!"

"No, you're right. Have a wank if you must."

"Yeah, right!!"

A few minutes later and it was my turn.

"Fuck you Callum! Bits of me are waking up!"

"Bits?"

"Okay, just the one bit if you must know, damn it!"

"Ignore it and try to get some sleep, or have a wank if you must!!"

*****

Eventually sleep did take centre stage and I didn't wake until gone ten the next morning. Callum was still out of it although he had managed to turn over in his sleep so now we were facing each other, our arms around each other's waists.

Actually, it was rather nice! It wasn't as if I could *feel* anything, we were still pretty much fully dressed, but being in such close contact with someone was new to me.

Before my mother got into drink and drugs, we used to share hugs and I missed those times but this? This was altogether better!

One of the young lads padded over towards us, a large overcoat draped around his shoulders.

"It's fucking cold in here. Can you do something with the fire?"

"What, and wake the sleeping beauty here? It'd be more than my life's worth!"

He studied Callum for a moment before turning to me.

"You really like him, don't you?"

"Yeah, I do. He's like, well special."

"I thought as much. I was awake when you turned over and cuddled up to him. Fuck, your faces were only inches apart and I was waiting for you to kiss him!"

"What? No, not like that like him? He's just a really good friend!"

"If you say so. He really likes you *like that* though!!"

"Piss off, Pip. Do the sodding fire if you must, but lay off me please?"

"Yeah, alright, but there's no shame if you do *really* like him you know? We all know he's gay and it's about time he found a boyfriend. He's really lonely, did you know that, Ed?"

"Em...... no, actually, I didn't. I see him as being confident and streetwise, but never lonely?"

"We have to put that across or people would walk all over us, but deep-down? We all have our problems, and short of giving ourselves up to the social services, the only people we can confide in is each other. We need each other just to get through the day. We might move around a lot so as not to get our collar's felt, but there's like a...... a bush telegraph what works well enough, so all of us know where we all are, that's how Callum managed to find us yesterday. Anyway, trust me. He's very lonely, so be good to him, okay?"

Chapter Three.

P ip tended the fire then came back over to talk to me. "Will you read to us again, Ed?"

"You liked the story then?"

"Well, yeah. We all of us did. Sometimes I get lucky and manage to slip in to a cinema, and that's cool, but it's kind of all set out for you, but last night, I dunno, it was like I could close my eyes and make up my own film set, places by the sea I went to when I was young, people I saw, the boats waiting out at sea, you know, waiting to come into harbour...... what you read to us sort of came to life somehow."

"Boats or ships?"

"What's the difference?"

"I'm not sure! They call submarines boats but they're huge some of them, yet coasters can be smaller and they're called ships."

"I once saw the film 'Das Boot", do you know it?"

"Yes. I read the book as well...... awesome! It was so weird the way they described the tension of the moment, the battle of wits and skill between the Captain of the British destroyer and the German U boat Commander, but told from the perspective of the Germans...... never come across that before."

"I know and it made me cry, the ending especially."

"Just goes to show that there's good inside everyone if you choose to look for it, I guess."

"Still got it?"

"The book? Don't think so, but if we could get into a library……?"

"I might know a way? Leave it with me!"

"Uh-uh! Too risky, and apart from anything else, that book is ages old and more than likely wouldn't be on the shelf now…… but if I could get on line.....?"

*****

Five days and two books later, the weather took a turn for the better. We never did get any snow which made moving around less of an issue, but what got to me was the fact that none of the kids were in any hurry to leave.

I pulled Callum to one side but his response was casual.

"We're lumbered with the little shits, and it's all down to you."

"Me? What did I do?"

"Read to them, fire their imagination, that's what? I can see just how much they love it, I feel the same way, but we've made a rod for our own backs here."

"But it's very risky them all being here, isn't it? What if we get sussed and the police come calling? Before, they would've netted the two of us, but now there's like nineteen of us."

"I wouldn't worry about it. If the police suspect anything, which I have to say is not likely, then they wouldn't expect to find a fucking army of kids, would they? No, maybe two or three so they wouldn't go off half-cocked and surround the place or send in a fucking swat team, they'd just send two or three, so most of the kids would make it out of here. What you've got to remember is that these kids know a thing or two about avoiding trouble, and anyway, they know the risks. If one of them did get picked up and put into care, you can bet your last penny they'd get the fuck out pretty bloody quick."

"Wouldn't they like, put them in prison?"

"For doing what exactly? What crime have they committed? So they're run-aways, so sodding what?"

Callum laughed. "There was one little lad who got picked up by the social services a while back, and he never even made it as far as a care home. This bloke and his woman assistant nabbed him and shoved him into their car so they could get him to a home, the doors were locked of course, but as they came to a set of lights, he told them he was going to puke. They opened the window and he was gone in a heartbeat, disappeared down an alleyway never to be seen by the social ever again! Any idea who that might've been?"

"You perhaps?"

"Nah, not me. Try Pip? He's got a brain in that head of his...... just a pity he won't ever get to make the most of it."

"Yes, I could see him pulling a stunt like that! Anyhow, that's the other thing. None of them are getting even a basic education and that's really sad."

"Well, you were looking for summat to occupy your time? Why don't you do something for them?"

"Me?"

"Yeah, grammar school boy, you. You're bright, I mean that's pretty obvious, so what if you were to say charge them a quid each per morning, that comes out at eighteen pounds a day as I count myself in as well, so what's that over a five day week, Ed?"

"Ninety quid. Not very much is it."

"It's better than the fuck-all you're bringing to the party right now!"

"Ouch!"

"Sorry, that was low even by my standards. You're a well special bloke and I wouldn't mind if you had to live here for nothing 'cos...... oh fuck it! I'd miss you if you left."

"Really??"

"Yeah, fucking really. Now shut the fuck up 'cos you're making me squirm!"

"Whoo-hoo! Is Callum getting all embarrassed then?"

"I thought I told you to shut up!"

"Yeah, and......?"

"Look, I happen to like you, like really, really like you, so now will you please, FUCKING SHUT UP!"

"Yeah. Okay. Shut-up mode is on."

Callum gave me the briefest of hugs then pushed me away, but the smile on his face spoke to me.

I studied his face before speaking.

"It's okay you know? I'm not made of glass?"

"Meaning what?"

"That hug. It was nice, and I thank you for it."

"You're welcome. Just make the most of it 'cos hugs isn't my speciality."

"That should read aren't, not isn't."

"Whatever...... schoolie!"

*****

That evening, as had now become routine, we mobbed Ronny's place, and seated upstairs and out of sight, we all pigged out on chicken, ham and leak pie, mashed potatoes and peas followed by a treacle pudding and custard. Ronny was charging us two pounds fifty per head, and the thought crossed my mind that he could hardly be covering his costs, so managing to find him in the kitchen, I decided to ask him.

"Look, Ronny, it's not like we're complaining but aren't you being over-generous? Seriously now, you can hardly be making a cent out of us at your prices?"

"I'm not even covering the cost of the food, but what you've got to remember is this, Ed. If you lot didn't scoff it, I'd have to chuck it out so a little is better than bugger-all."

"Yes, well, but even so......"

"Listen to me for a moment. I've got kids back home and me and the missus try to give them a decent life. You kids, well, you're a different matter. On your uppers, no real future worth a wank, like a lost generation, and like as not, through no fault of your own. Sure, I could turn you away, call the law or whatever, but the way I see it is, what good would it do? You'd only run away again."

"You don't extend your good-will to those adults out there, well not that I'm aware of?"

"No, I don't. I'm not some bloody drop-in centre for every drug addict, drunk or mental case, the state should do their bit when it comes to them, but lack of funding, shortage of trained staff, or if my guess is correct, just plain disinterest, means nothing gets done."

"Sorry if I've over-stepped the mark. None of my business what you do or why you do it."

"Don't worry about it, Ed. So long as you're all fed and watered, I can rest easy in my bed safe in the knowledge that I've done my best by you."

*****

Back in our garret we began settling in to an evening of story-telling, but before I started, I put Callum's idea of schooling to the kids.

"Well, that's about the size of it. As I see it, none of us have much of a future to look forward to, and without the basics like reading, writing and some mathematics under your belt, nobody would even think about offering you work. So, who's up for it then?"

There was a brief exchange of conversation before one by one, they cautiously raised their hands. Tigger voiced one concern however.

"We'll need paper and pencils and you don't even have a blackboard Ed."

"Yes, I know. So, we've got a few logistical problems, but nothing we can't sort between us. Let's get back to the story and over the next couple of days, give some thought to how we might get this show on the road."

*****

Two days on, Malc and Tiny tuned up puffing and sweating under the weight of a large cardboard box.

"That looks interesting?"

"We think it is! Wait 'till you see what we've managed to thieve."

Malc opened the box and inside were a pile of lined exercise books, a couple of reams of white A4 size card, a box of white chalk and another that contained an assortment of coloured ones. To top it all, they'd managed to find a couple of boxes of pencils, some rulers, erasers, pencil sharpeners and a blackboard wiper.

"Shit, you blokes? Where on earth did you get this lot from?"

"You don't need to know that! Let's just say that this place had left a skylight open, Tiny managed to get in and open a down stairs window so we rifled the contents of the storeroom. I bet they'll be surprised 'cos we left a whole load of laptops behind!"

Tiny chirped up and looking disgruntled muttered,

"Yeah and we could've flogged those and made us some money."

I thought about his comment for a moment.

"Maybe something to think about for another time. Computer skills are very important, but if you can't even read or write, computers will be useless to you. All we need to get started is a blackboard, so got any ideas?"

"Best you have a word with Callum, I think he's working on something out the back."

*****

I found Callum outside on his hands and knees painting the sheet of hardboard he'd used to block off the fireplace.

"Once I've finished painting, this'll be your blackboard. I em........borrowed a tin of bitumen from next door together with a paint brush, so with a bit of luck and all assuming it don't piss down overnight, it'll be dry by the morning."

"Nice work! Hey, if it's not dry, I could always use you, you look like a fucking nigger!"

"Don't use that word, it's disrespectful."

"Oh, I'm so very sorry, *rent boy?"*

"Fucking ex-rent boy, retired rent boy even."

"Oh, yeah? Since when!"

"Since the last time you gave me grief...... if you must know!"

"Why? I mean, I'm really, *really* pleased but......"

"Why? It upset you, that's sodding why?"

"Yeah, you're right, it did. You're very special and you deserve something better than selling your...... cute body. Look, I know you made a stack of cash doing it, but honest to Christ, Callum? I need you, want you to be around, so given that you could catch all sorts of hideous infections, I don't want your money and neither do I want to find myself hiding behind a tree in some cemetery, watching as they bury your remains six foot under."

"So, I'm cute now, am I?" He grinned.

"Yeah well, I only get to see you undressed twice a week at the swimming pool when we take a shower, and then there are other people about, so...... hang a-fucking-bout? What are you trying to say here? Are you suggesting that I perve on you?"

"Well I perve on *you,* so why not?"

"You're bad, did you know that?"

"Yep! Bad's my middle name, haha!"

"Fuck you!"

"I used to charge a fortune for that, but…… beings as it's you…… no charge, Ed!"

I knelt down beside him and leaning over, I kissed him on the forehead.

"God, Callum? You can be a real twatt sometimes!"

*****

Story time over for another night, so as Pip tended the fire, I spoke to the assembled.

"Looks like we'll be ready to rock by tomorrow morning, guys. Those of you who are still up for a bit of education, can we say, get breakfast done and dusted, then once any little jobs are out of the way, we can make a start.

Any questions?"

Charlie stuck up his hand.

"Ed? Will you be caning us if we mess up?"

"Fuck no! What brought that question on, Cha?"

"Nuffin'? I was just wonderin'?"

A voice from one of the boxes spoke up.

"He's disappointed! Charlie loves a bit of S&M, don't you, Cha!"

"Fuck off, Abe. I don't go tellin' about your, um…… specialities, do I?"

"I guess. Chill out, Cha? Only kidding you?"

"You're forgiven. I'm knackered so I'm going to hit the sack…… or should that read, newspapers."

Another voice from another box.

"Yeah, well it would do if you could actually fuckin' read!"

Charlie rolled his eyes and grinning at me, whispered, "He's right, but you're going to take care of that, aren't you, Ed?"

"Going to give it my best shot, Cha. Go and get some sleep, okay?"

"Yeah. Good night, Ed."

Chapter Four.

Over the weeks, I'd called the hospital but with much the same response. 'Sorry, but we're unable to give out details of someone's condition unless you're a close family member.'

I decided to break cover and use my own phone, but first I needed to get away for a couple of hours, somewhere away from here where my signal wouldn't be traced back.

I decided to tell Callum.

"Can you come with me?"

"I could, but I'm not going to, Ed. You need Pip on this jaunt, not me. Do you want me to talk to him for you?"

"Thanks, but why not you?"

"I only know this locality whereas Pip has been all over, knows the bus routes and so on, so no, you stick with him and his local knowledge."

*****

I really liked Pip. He was younger than me by around seven months, nice looking, articulate and funny, but what set him apart was that he seemed to have eyes up his arse.

He steered me through side streets and back alleyways, all the time telling me what to avoid and why, and alright, I could see why Callum trusted his judgement.

"You know the city pretty well Pip."

"Yeah. My Dad was a taxi driver, and before you had all the Pakki's chasing around in their private hire cars, you had to take a test like they do in London."

"I never knew that. Carry on?"

"Well, in London they call it *The Knowledge,* but it was much the same in Brum, like you had to understand the shortest routes from A to B and not just in one area of town, it was like all over. Anyway, when he was learning it, he'd take me with him and keep up like a running commentary...... most of it sort of stuck with me I suppose."

"You loved your Dad, right?"

"Yeah, I adored him!"

"So...... what happened to him?"

"A truck, a fuck-off massive truck sandwiched him into a wall...... killed him outright."

"That's terrible, mate. What about you're Mum?"

"She died giving birth to my brother some years earlier...... he didn't survive either, so I was fostered out. I was a problem child, I suppose, so I got shoved from pillar to post. I got pissed off big time so I did a runner, and well, here I am."

"I'm sorry."

"Don't be. Stuff happens and you learn to deal with it, but just a word of caution, don't be in any rush to go quizzing the others as to why they're on the streets, okay? Some of their stories would make your toes curl. They'll tell you if they feel comfortable around you, but...... you get my point, yeah?"

"Yes, I hear you.

Can I tell you something, Pip?"

"Sure...... just so long as it's not too personal!"

"Before I ran away, I always got the impression that life on the streets was a lonely existence, you know the sort of thing, constantly on the move, never meeting anyone or forming close friendships, but I got it all wrong. At school I had friends, not what you might call close, but sort of casual, but now? Having been on the streets for only around two months, I know so many people, people such as yourself, Callum, Malc, Tiny, Tigger and Paulie, all of which I feel much closer to than any of those kids at school. The other thing is, it's been a long time since I've felt this happy. It's really hard to explain 'cos I don't have all the luxuries I used to, almost sod-all money, living each day as it comes and all without the stability and security of a home life, yet I feel alive!"

Pip chuckled. "I know what you mean! Maybe this lifestyle agrees with you. There are plenty of kids that just can't hack it and end up turning themselves in, but in your case, you did have one big break in as much as you came across Callum. Callum's not all sweetness and light, I mean, fucking-hell, that is so far from the truth as he lives by his own standards, which I have to say, aren't as high as they might be, but one thing he does have going for him is that if he likes you, and trust me, Ed, he *really* likes you...... what I'm trying to say is, he would never, not ever crap on a friend. He has, what's the word, integrity, his word is his bond.

Now, what might've happened had you not met him you'll never know, but things might've been completely different and *you* might have been one of those kids turning themselves in."

"Yes, I know you're right, but what I still find fascinating is, I've gone from having a few decent enough friends to having a lot of what I look upon as close mates, and all in the space of two months. It's as if I live with an enormous family."

"This winter is the first time that's happened. Sure, we used to shelter together when the weather was shit, but then everyone would go their separate ways. You'd see them around from time to time then maybe get together again the following winter, but that's about it. You've got your story-telling to thank for that!"

We walked on a bit further then suddenly Pip took hold of my hand and pulled me into an alleyway.

"Trouble?"

"No, but it's as well to get a move on. Don't worry, we're almost there."

A few minutes later and Pip took us through into a sort of courtyard. "We'll be okay here, but before you make your call, I'll be keeping a watchful eye on things and if I whistle you, drop what you're doing and follow me, stick to me like a magnet, okay?"

"Got it!"

I fired up my phone. Six missed calls, and on checking the numbers, two were from school friends, two were withheld numbers and the other two I didn't recognise, but there was no voicemail so I called the hospital.

"Good morning. My name is Edward Anderson. Could you put me through to Ward Twenty please?"

This time I did get answers. My mother had been transferred to the Good Hope Hospital in Aston. She had recovered sufficiently to enable her to go into detox but not before being sectioned under the Mental Health Act.

A further call to Good Hope revealed that once the doctors were satisfied that she was sufficiently clean, she'd be transferred to a secure psychiatric unit for appraisal, and depending on the outcome, they'd make their decision.

At no time did they mention her man friend, and I wasn't about to go asking, however the Ward Sister at Good Hope told me that mother had written me a letter and either I could go there and collect it or they would post it to me.

Risky I know, but I elected to take the post option telling them to send it to our Solihull address.

"I'm done here Pip. Thanks for the guided tour!"

"No worries, but just make sure you turn that phone off!"

Rather than taking the same torturous route of earlier, this time involved a straight forward bus trip to within half a mile of our hideaway where we once again took to the side streets and alleyways. On the bus Pip asked me how things were with my mother.

"Well enough, I guess. She's been sectioned, and once she's done with detox they'll evaluate her, but what happens after that is anyone's guess."

"So, where is she right now?"

"Good Hope Hospital in Aston."

"Ha! My dad used to call it the No Hope Hospital!"

"How come?"

"'Cos that's where my Mum died. For Christ's sake, Ed? It's a hospital specifically set up for women, and they can't even get to deliver a fucking baby without bolloxing it up!"

"I'm sorry."

"Don't be. All water under the bridge. Let the dead bury their own dead, blah-di-blah."

"Very profound."

"Uh-uh. Very Bible!"

"Religious then?"

"Me? Religious? Get out of town, Ed! If, and I say, *IF* there was a God up there, why is it we got ourselves such a crap life?

Suffer little children to come unto me? Suffer little children, more like!"

"That's funny!"

"Yeah, well, you've got to laugh at life or you'd go nuts."

"Talking of favours which we weren't, I might be asking you for another one."

"Go on?"

"The nurse at Good Hope told me my mother had written me a letter. She told me I could go and collect it, not an option, either that or she'd put it in the post."

"And?"

"I need to get back to Solihull and I'd like you with me, simply put, I need your eyes and ears on this one."

"Yeah, okay, I'm in. When do you want to go?"

"Day after tomorrow. That should give enough time for that letter to arrive even if they sent it second class."

"Day after tomorrow. Shit, Ed? That's Monday! Well risky!"

"Yeah but I've got me a cunning plan! Have you got a decent pair of trousers?"

"Yep. I nicked a pair only last week. Really posh, like charcoal grey."

"Perfect! If you were to borrow one of my school shirts and my school tie, I could wear my grey slacks and school blazer, so just two lads out of school!"

"Yeah, but what if we're seen? If one of your teacher's saw you, there'd be hell to pay."

"Not necessarily? We go there out of school hours like early evening. There's a short cut over the recreation ground that leads to the back of my house and bingo!"

"And getting back afterwards?"

"That's the clever part. We stay there overnight, it'll be warm and the chance to get cleaned up, then we disappear at first light back the way we came."

"Okay, but what if we get stopped?"

"In the morning? Simple. We tell whoever it is that we're on our way to Birmingham International to meet an exchange student off a flight from France then take him back to our school."

"Alright, it seems like you've got all bases covered. Solihull, here we come."

*****

Monday evening found us on the train. Bad timing meant we had to stand for the entire journey, but with each of us carrying backpacks full of books, we looked for all the world like two very average schoolboys and we were never approached.

Inside the house, it became obvious that no one had set foot over the threshold as there was a massive amount of post on the mat by the front door, the central heating was still running and everything was how I'd left it two months ago. I rifled through the assortment of letters and bills, probably all final demands, but then found what we'd come for. A letter with my name written in my mother's handwriting, then our address in a different hand.

"Pip? If you fancy taking a hot bath, then go help yourself. I think I wanna be on my own when I read this 'cos if she gets all mushy, the waterworks will take me over!"

"Ooo, yeah! The luxury of a warm bath! I'm gone!"

I tore open the envelope and studied the contents.

> *'Edward. I have no idea where you are or what you might be doing but I can only assume you are short of money*
> *Rolling Stones Emotional Rescue 5131.*
> *Your mother.'*

Short and to the point, but what the fuck is she on about?

I waited until Pip reappeared.

"So? Good new or bad?"

"Dunno. I'll read it to you."

"Look, Ed? If it's like, personal? I mean, it's none of my business."

"Personal? It's business-like plus I don't understand it!"

"Okay then, let's hear it."

I read it out loud, then turning to Pip, I begged the obvious.

"Well then? Any idea what she's banging on about?"

"Rolling Stones. A rock band yeah?"

"And?"

"Emotional Rescue was one of their albums, pretty good actually."

"Thanks for the tutorial in contemporary music, but what about it?"

"Did your Mum have a music collection?"

"Yes, but it's scattered all over the lounge floor. It'd be like looking for a needle in a haystack."

"So, we'd better get started then. Shake a leg, Ed?"

Two hours on and nothing, but then I found the CD sleeve but no CD.

"Anything in the sleeve?"

"No, it's empty. This a fucking waste of time, Pip."

"Wait up a minute. She went to all the bother of writing to you and then kind of coded something. Why would she do that if there was no rhyme or reason behind it?"

"God only knows."

"Let's start from scratch.

She writes to you. She mentions a particular rock band. Not only that, she mentions one Rolling Stones album out of the dozen or so we've found. We find said album or more specifically, the sleeve for said album, so what does that tell us?"

"I don't fucking know!!"

"If you find an empty album cover, where might you find the album?

"In the........."

"Hoo-fucking-ray! Open up the CD player and see if there's anything inside."

I plugged the machine into a wall socket and opened up the player.

Inside was the CD, but that looked to be it, and feeling as if I'd been betrayed, I went to lift it out so I could throw it across the room, but as I did so, I noticed that it hadn't been clipped into position.

Now why I felt the need to clip it into place is something I'll never fully understand, but as hard as I tried, the pissing thing just *wouldn't* sit in so I lifted it out, and the reason behind it became clear.

On the underside of the disc, a debit card had been taped in place, but no ordinary debit card this, it was a Lloyds Bank Premier card.

"Well I'll be damned! Take a gander at this Pip?"

"So, it's a bank card. Not much use without the...... 5131!! That has to be the PIN!!"

"Yes, but......"

"Yes, but what?"

"Yes, but the name on the card is Vincent Conner."

"So? I take it that's your Mum's boyfriend."

"Yes, and therein lies the problem."

"Please will you stop talking in riddles Ed? What's the issue here?"

"There's not going to be any money on it. That fucker stole my bank book, presumably to back his various habits, so it stands to reason, he'd run out of his own."

"Then why would your Mum go hiding it?"

"Search me. All this way, two bloody train tickets and all the risks involved, and for what?"

"I dunno, but something inside me says different. Did this Vincent bloke have a mobile phone?"

"Yes. It's most likely upstairs in the main bedroom. What do we want it for?"

"Check it for messages."

"I'll go and see if I can find it. Do you want to go and make us some coffee?"

"Okay. Also it might be an idea to open the rest of the post while we're here."

*****

I found the phone but the battery was as flat as a pancake, so over coffee I set it on charge and between us we went through the post.

This mostly comprised of junk mail and final demands. There were a couple of hospital appointment reminders, but otherwise nothing of significance.

"No bank statements, Ed. Wouldn't you have expected to see at least one after two months?"

"Probably not. Mother did her banking electronically, maybe he did as well."

"I haven't noticed a computer anywhere though."

"They used my laptop, but then they kicked the crap out of it."

"How's that phone looking?"

"Three parts charged. Good enough for what we need it for. I'll check for messages."

To begin with there was nothing of interest. Most of the callers had just hung up, but then, with only six messages remaining, we hit the jackpot.

"Fucking-hell Pip! Talk about heavyweight. Listen to this. I'll put it on speaker."

"Who's a bad boy then, Vince. A very, *very bad boy!* You had the stuff and I *know* you've offloaded it, so where's my money?

This is very much last chance saloon for you, my son, and so if you don't come up with the full amount by tomorrow night, then quicker than you can say crack cocaine, you'll find yourself propping up a fucking motorway bridge.

Don't mess with me Vincent. This is no idle threat!"

Chapter Five.

"Y ou mustn't touch it Ed, you do realise that, don't you?"

"Yes, I know, but what the fuck *do* I do? I get some coded shit message from my mother who, by the way, used to hit me, throw furniture and plates at me and obviously couldn't give a flying fuck about me, I end up with a very dodgy bank card that gives me access to a fucking fortune, and unless we collectively have totally misread the situation, what I'm sitting on is drug money, probably owed to some animal who would slit your throat sooner than look at you."

"A tad melodramatic but point taken."

"*Melodramatic Callum??* This is the stuff of movies!"

"Yeah, okay. Try to calm down 'cos panicking never solved shit."

*****

Pip and I had talked through into the wee small hours before collapsing onto my mother's bed at three in the morning. We agreed that what had come out of that voicemail had to be reported, but how to get around the problem of opening up to the police and risk being taken into care was top of our agenda.

Before finally succumbing to sleep, I tucked Vincent's phone and charger into my back pack together with the debit card, then the following morning at six o'clock, we were waiting none to patiently at Solihull station and the first train of the day that would get us back to Moor Street and the safety of our hideaway.

Once in the station concourse, we found an ATM and shoved the card in the slot. The PIN worked and rather than looking at the on-screen balance, I chose Mini-Statement, removed the card, never bothering to look at the balance, then made our way back to our alleyway hideout.

*****

"I'm not panicking, I'm fucking scared!"

"Then let your adrenaline work positively for you, Ed? Who would you normally turn to in times of trouble…… sorry, that was a stupid question."

"No, it isn't? I used to turn to my Dad, but how I find him is the problem."

"Discount it. He fucked off and abandoned you so you don't even know if you can trust him."

"Clergy?"

"You're not a church-goer."

"No, but they live by a certain standard, don't they?"

Pip giggled. "So does Callum, remember?"

I laughed. "Yeah, but that's different. I trust you blokes, you're my closest friends, and hell, you probably even remember the PIN number, you could help yourself to the lot but…… I know you'd never do that."

"Nice…… and no, I wouldn't even dream about doing such a thing. I nick stuff as and when I need it. It's a bit like Tiny and Malc thieving from that school. They left the computers only taking what was needed to set up our classroom. Steal to survive."

"There's always that anonymous crime reporting line?"

"Is there? Not caught up with that?"

"Yep, it's like, a Freephone number, 0800 or something. You can dial it and report something suspicious without having to give out your personal details."

"Yes, but that still leaves me with a slight problem. I've got evidence that I'd have to hand over, and how do you go about that anonymously?"

Callum squeezed my shoulder. "First off, this is *our* problem, not just yours. Yes, okay, you are firmly sitting on the front line but you mustn't think you're on your own."

I smiled at him and returned the shoulder squeeze. "Yeah, I know it. One other thing to take into account, is that I accessed that voicemail so now it'll only be saved for seven days, so whatever decision I, sorry, *we* come t,o has to be done pretty bloody quickly."

"If we've not decided after tonight, then we've been dragging our feet. Actually, I'm in favour of this 0800 lark. Can we take a vote?"

*****

"Hi. My name is…… forget it…… sorry! Are you a police officer?"

"No, I'm a call handler."

"I need to speak with a policeman."

"Tell me what it's all about, and then, depending on the nature of your call, you might find yourself doing just that."

"Drugs…… well, I think this is what it's all about?"

"Have you been offered drugs?"

"No, but I've got evidence that it's going on."

"Unfortunately, you can buy whatever takes your fancy just about anywhere. What specifically are we talking about here?"

"This isn't about your average pusher, I'm talking supply on a fucking industrial scale."

"Hold the line please."

How long can it take?? I waited for what seemed like a lifetime, so long was it, I even checked Callum's battery level, but then finally, I got to speak to a *real policeman!*

"I'm Detective Inspector Tony Bushby, Birmingham City Police Drug Squad. Who am I talking to please?"

"What? Oh, alright. My name is immaterial, Fred Immaterial, if you must know. Fucking-hell? I phone a number that promises anonymity, and the first question you ask is my fucking name?? What's going on here?"

"Settle down, son. We are fed calls from various sources, I honestly didn't realise. How can I help you?"

I ran him through as much detail as I could without disclosing names and addresses, but shit, I almost blew it on a number of occasions!

"How much did you say was lodged on that account?"

"Wait a second and I'll tell you down to the last penny......
one million three hundred and thirty-five thousand pounds give or take."

"Give or take?"

"Sorry, but I'm very frightened...... just my way of defusing things. The amount I mentioned is correct."

Our DCI whistled down the phone.

"We need to see that card so we can access that bank account, but what's even more important is to get a handle on that voice-mail, in short, we need that phone."

"Yes, I realise that, but how do I get it to you?"

"You could come to a Police Station or we could collect it from you."

"Neither option is an option."

"May I ask why?"

"I live rough, I'm a street kid and I can't risk arrest or the Social Services getting involved."

"A vagrant?"

"Not a term I'd like to use, but if it floats your boat……"

"Okay, okay…… What if I promised you that there wouldn't be any arrests or involvement of any outside agencies, how might you feel about that?"

"I'd need guarantees."

"I don't know how we go about that. What if I said that I would meet you at any time and at a place of your choosing? How would you feel about that?"

"Call me back in thirty minutes. You've got the number?"

"Yes, I've logged it. I'll get back to you."

*****

"Oh, Jesus, Ed? You definitely know how to kick at a fucking rat's nest, don't you?"

Callum was sitting squat-legged by the canal, head in his hands.

Pip rounded on him.

"For fuck's sake, Callum? For a guy who professes to hold a candle for Ed, you sure as shit don't show it too well?"

I heard but I didn't listen.

I think I knew but……

"Yeah, well, this is serious. One step out of place and……"

"And what! We have to get this junk to the police, even you know that, so shut the fuck up and let me think!"

I touched Callum on the arm.

"Hold a candle for me?"

He looked up at me, and for the first time I saw behind the façade, a young and vulnerable Callum was looking into my eyes, but the moment was short lived as Pip re-joined us.

"Got a plan. What kicks off beginning on Friday?"

"Em…… the German Christmas market. What of it?"

"Got it in one! This market could prove to be a God send. Nice and busy, and loads of kids will be there come Saturday, but for my idea to work will mean that all of us will have to be in the loop, not just us three."

Callum perked up.

"Go on?"

"My first thought was to arrange a meet some place out in the open, like a park where there weren't too many people floating about.

My thinking was that if the law decided to go back on their word and shit on us, we'd see them coming a mile off giving us time to do a runner. Yeah, that might've worked, but then I got to thinking. What if we used people to confuse the issue? If we waited 'till Saturday, the city centre will be mobbed with mum's, dad's, shit loads of kids and tourists which gives us perfect cover. What we do is get everyone to mingle with the crowds, the police wouldn't be able to tell the difference between one of us from any other kid, we stay close enough to give out a warning, so if we get raided, we just melt away into the crowd and the deal's off.

That's the first bit but I like the second bit best!

This guy Bushby would expect to be meeting Ed, but actually, Ed will be meeting him!"

"What's the difference?"

"The difference, Callum, is this. Ed tells him where to go and what to wear, something that makes him stand out. That way we all recognise him, but he hasn't got a fucking clue what any of us look like, and so once we're happy that he's not come mob-handed, Ed finds him, hands the stuff over before losing himself in the throng.

Am I a genius or am I a genius?!"

I laughed. "That's so good it just might work!"

Callum got to his feet. "Well, you've come up with a fair few scams in your time, Pip, but even by your high standards, that's a fucking cracker!"

"Call it my Christmas Cracker!"

*****

"Did he call you back as promised?"

"Yes, and I told him to be at the fountain in St Stephen's Square at two-thirty Saturday afternoon. He's going to call back in the next day or so to tell me what he'll be wearing. Oh, yeah, I also told him that he wasn't calling my phone, and if you picked up the call, that was okay as you knew all about it."

"Was he alright about stuff?"

"Not really. I got the feeling he's used to dictating terms rather than the other way 'round!"

"Well, fuck him. You've got something he wants, he might even get to solve a big crime and get promotion, so it makes sense for him to play ball just this once."

"Can I ask you for a favour, Callum?"

"Ask away."

"If we're going to involve the others, we've got to get them onside, and I just thought it might be better coming from you, you know, give them the big brother talk."

"Yeah, okay. When do you want me to do it?"

"Sooner rather than later, so how's about tonight before story-time? We can pretty much guarantee they'll all be there. No need to go into detail, just the basics."

*****

Callum had set out our stall rather well I thought, but given the sort of life we followed, there were always going to be a few dissenters.

"I don't like the idea of shopping someone to the cops. Sort of goes against the grain somehow."

"Yeah, I hear you Mitch, and given most normal circumstances I'd be right there with you but this is far from being normal. We're not talking about some petty criminal thing here, what we're looking at is something of epic proportions, not only that, this has put Ed in a *very* bad place, so if it makes you feel better, try not to think on this as helping the police, think of it as helping Ed, okay?"

"Alright already."

"Look, we've thought long and hard about this. It's taken a master scammer to come up with a plan that should keep all of us out of trouble, so are we agreed?"

Mitch grinned. "By master scammer, you have to be talking a Pip scam, right?"

"In one!"

"In that case, I'm in."

"Nice one, Mitch! Right. There is one last item on the agenda before I hand over to Ed for story-time, and I have to insist on your undivided attention, so fucking-well pay attention.

The German market runs right the way up to the New Year, yeah? Plenty of time to do whatever it is you do, *BUT......* this Saturday there must be no shenanigans, no fucking about and you must do nothing to bring unwanted attention from the cops. Put one foot out of line and I promise you, you'll live to regret it. Any of you get arrested then you won't be allowed back here, got it?"

A little voice from the back of the room.

"Would you really kick us out?"

"No...... I couldn't do that, but fuck-up on this and I'll have your guts for garters. Remember, we're doing this to help one of our own and we never, ever, shit on our own doorstep, do we!"

Chapter Six.

The weather, given it was December and Christmas just around the corner, was still on the parky side although nowhere near as cold as it had been two weeks before.

Our respective boxes still had tenants in residence which meant that Callum and I still shared sleeping bags. We had gone from using just one to zipping two together giving us space to turn over without necessarily disturbing each other. I don't know why we hadn't gone back to the old arrangement of separate bags...... well I do now, but back then? When we were ready for sleep, we'd turn away from each other, but why we woke come the morning almost on top of each other was weird, but a nice, cosy weird!

The night before the meet, we were doing our normal chatting when I thought struck me.

"Hey, Callum? Did you ever watch that program on telly called The A Team?"

"Yeah! I loved it!"

"Well, it's like we've got our own A Team right here in this room."

"Really? And what makes you think that?"

"Think about it for a moment. You *have* to be the leader, the Colonel, what was his name...... Hannibal Smith, was it? Pip has to be Face, you know, like the schemer, the ideas man, the charmer of the bunch, then you've got Malc and Tiny, I mean they seem to be able to get hold of almost anything so they must be B.A. Barrachus!"

"But then there's you. You haven't left yourself much wriggle-room, therefore you *have to be* Mad Murdoch!!"

"Ah, fuck it, I must be mad if only for choosing to live like this!"

"Ed?"

"Yeah?"

"Can I have a hug? Just a quickie?"

I drew him into me and gave him a cuddle, only about three or four seconds, but then he kissed me on the nose and pushing me away smiling, said, "I love it when a plan comes together!!"

*****

So as not to draw attention to themselves, the kids left in dribs and drabs, making their way to St Stephen's Square with Pip, Callum and I following on close behind.

Callum had again gone over the 'what to do and what not to do' so many times that none of them could've been in any doubt as to what was expected of them.

For the three of us, it was different. Once I'd spotted Mr Bushby and having received no warning signals, I was to approach him and do the business. Pip and Callum would casually follow me and sit as close to us as they could without rousing any suspicions, the idea being, if something were to kick off, they'd be there to spirit me away, but as things turned out, there was no need for concern.

Mr Bushby turned up dot on time but with a lady and two children in tow.

I had to smile as he, and both the kids were sporting reindeer antlers, just as he had told me!

"Mr Bushby?"

"Hello, son. Just let me say, this is my rest day, no one knows I'm here, no one has come with me except my family, so you've no need to be concerned, alright?"

"Thanks for that, but you understand why I have to be careful?"

"Yes. I just wish things were different for you."

"I'm doing okay. You want the gear, I guess?"

"Please."

"Here you go. The bank card. Have you got a pen?

The PIN is 5131.

One Samsung Galaxy S4 together with charger. Can I go now?"

"Of course? You're not under arrest after all, but please...... just spare me a moment more?"

"Okay, but my friends will be getting twitchy."

He grinned. "I've been surrounded have I?"

"Big time, but I bet you can't see them."

"No need, no interest, but I do need to tell you a few things, things that might help you."

"Like?"

"Like...... I know who you are, where you lived, what school you attended, do you want me to continue?"

My mouth went dry and I had this burning desire to burst into tears...... so I did! Pip must've counted to five before he was up on his feet, then confronted Mr Bushby head on.

"Hey, hey, hey! What's going on? Leave the kid alone, you pervert? Jesus H., you guys ought to be castrated, you know that?"

"I, I, it's nothing like that! We were just talking!"

Pip looked at me and winked. "Well, just so long as that's all you're doing it." Then looking at me with a straight face, "You okay, mate? Want us to call the law or anything?"

I tried very hard to keep control of my giggles.

"I'm fine but thanks...... thanks anyway, mate."

After Pip sat back down next to Callum, Mr Bushby looked somewhat shocked.

"One of yours?"

I nodded. "Yeah. One of the best."

"Do you think they'd come over and join us for a minute?"

I beckoned them over. They looked at each other, shrugged their shoulders and came over.

Bushby continued.

"You had me shitting myself there! Nice to see a spirit of camaraderie though. I've just told Edward that A, we know who he is, and B, where he lived, C, we know where he went to school, and D...... where he stays now, but please, please don't worry yourselves. I'm a senior Police Officer whose only concern is to nail those who traffic drugs. Yes, of course petty crime is wrong, but my time is limited enough as things stand, so my interest in you is purely humanitarian. Stay safe, and if possible, out of trouble, and just one final thing? Phones. It really doesn't make any difference whether your phone is PAYG or contract. Your address is of no consequence because every mobile has a signature, and once we know the caller I.D. we are able to latch onto it and trace you to within around five hundred feet.

Again, don't worry. None of your phones are being tapped or traced and no calls are being intercepted.

Now, run along, meet up with your friends and buy them all a hot drink on me.

Edward? I'll be in touch."

*****

"That was almost surreal! I'm talking to cop, a senior bloody cop at that! Jesus, Ed? The places life takes you!"

"Yes well...... what I want to know is where the next stop is. Did the lads do okay do you know? Any defaulters or problems?"

"Not that I'm aware of. They did pretty well considering all the temptations around them."

I turned to Pip. "You were fantastic! How on earth did you come up with that stunt?"

"What stunt?"

"The bloody 'what the fuck pervert' thing, you idiot!"

"Oh, right! Well, I really was worried, you know? Of course, I knew well enough he wasn't a pervert, but then he didn't know I knew that, so I just went for it, I guess.

It was fun!"

Both Callum and I burst out laughing, and as if with one voice shouted, 'FACE!'

"What??"

"Nothing...... private joke already!"

Pip shook his head then grinned. "Fucking head-cases, the pair of you!

*****

None of our kids had transgressed, none of them had come back with dodgy goods and none had been arrested, so just before story-time, I thanked them.

"Cheers for this afternoon, guys, I mean, I know you must've been tempted to take full advantage of the situation, but you all did me one massive kindness, and I won't forget it in a hurry. I still can't let on why I had to do what I did, but safe to say, that bloke I met up with is a pretty high-ranking policeman. There's no need to freak out, everything's cool, just go about your lives as normal and everything will be cushtie."

*****

I read until the torch gave out, then after Pip tended the fire, we all bedded down for the night.

I'd only managed to read for around three-quarters of an hour, which was frustrating. Maybe I could've carried on using the light from the fire, but my eyes were sore as it was.

"What I wouldn't give for electric light. Reading by torch light is okay but it's putting a strain on my eyes and besides, we're eating batteries and they don't come cheap."

"Get some of the kids to nick some then...... but that won't help your eyes, will it."

"No, it won't, and anyway, is that your solution to everything, steal it?"

"Pretty much? Alright, at the moment we have some money, but it isn't like a bottomless pit, Ed?"

"I know it. Now, if you wanted them to nick summat useful, get them to nick a generator!"

"Why?"

"Try, generate our own electricity maybe?"

"But we've already got one."

"What?? Where! I've never seen one? Why didn't you mention this before?"

"'Cos I think it's fucked."

"What makes you think that?"

"I got it to run once but it sounded like a pile of shit, plus the pissing thing scared the pants off me!"

"You'll have to show me in the morning."

"Yeah, sure, but I think it's a lost cause to be honest.

C'mon, let's get some sleep."

*****

"There you go? One totally totalled generator!"

"Jesus! I wondered why this passageway always reeked of diesel? Now I know why, and anyhow, that's not a generator, it's a fucking museum piece!"

"Not in the first flush of youth, I grant you!"

"Any sign of an instruction manual?"

"There was one…… if I can but remember what I did with it. Hang on, I'll go have a ferret about."

Callum was back with me a few minutes later.

"Found it. Don't know if all the pages are there though."

"Let's take it outside so we can get a better look at it."

*****

"Bollinder Crude Oil Engines, Eskilstuna, Sweden. I was right, it *is* a bloody museum piece! They sold out to Volvo just shortly after the war!

Water cooled single cylinder two stroke heavy oil engine ideally suited for many applications including blah – blah – blah…… did you say it ran rough?"

"Terminally so. It sort of farted and coughed a lot, blew loads of smoke out of the exhaust then the revs went up to the point where I took cover just in case it exploded!"

"I don't think that should've happened! It says here that the maximum working revolutions should be limited to three hundred, your average car ticks over at around eight hundred if memory serves, so this old girl should run really slowly."

"Uh-uh. That beast was going like full chat. Scared the living crap out of me it did!

You carry on reading and I'll make us some coffee."

*****

"Okay then. I reckon I've got a handle on it. Actually, even though I'm no engineer, it's pretty simple. Can you show me what you did to get it running?"

"I probably did it all wrong 'cos all I could do was look at the pictures, I can't read remember? First there was this one. It shows a sight glass, and that arrow there I thought must be the lowest level for the engine oil, so I hopped next door and…… borrowed some and filled it right to the top.

Next picture shows some bloke with his foot on a peg sticking out of what I guessed was the flywheel, and the next picture shows him kicking the engine over.

I tell you, it fucking nearly killed me. It took me ages to even get any sign of life out of it!"

"Yes, but there's a page missing, so maybe you missed something. They say something about a glowing taper that should be screwed into the top of the cylinder head, so let's go take a closer look."

*****

"Fuck this! We need a generator to fix the generator! I can hardly see a thing in this light!"

"I'll go get the torch shall I?"

"The batteries are dead, remember?"

"Ha-ha! So they are! Silly me!"

We did eventually find the taper holder, unscrewing it was some something of a challenge, but with the aid of a large stone and a lump of wood, we managed to free it off and remove it. Other bits that needed attention included the fuel tank which had rusted through in places, but the lower half was still in one piece so probably good enough to hold something at least. All the unions attaching the fuel line to the engine were loose which probably accounted for the stench of fuel, so we needed spanners, but aside from that, it looked okay to me.

At ten o'clock we abandoned it in favour of schooling, but in the afternoon we returned to it having had time to think.

"So, what do we need these taper-things for, Ed?"

"I think the idea is that they warm the fuel making it easier to ignite, but where or how we get hold of any, God only knows."

"Let me go see if Pip's still around, maybe he'll come up with something."

Ten minutes later and I began to wonder if Callum had been kidnapped but then he reappeared.

"Pip went into town, something about needing to call in a favour, but Buba doesn't think he'll be very long.

Any further forward?"

"A bit. The engine isn't seized which was my biggest worry, but until we work out how we heat the fuel, we'll be doing what you did like bust a gut getting it to fire."

"Never again sunshine.

Do you really understand how these things work or is it pure guess work?"

"Ha! Pure guess work! I once took our old petrol mower to bits to find out how it worked."

"Well, that's something at least?"

"Is it? The sodding thing never did work again. My Dad threw a fit!"

"Did you learn anything from it?"

"Oh, yeah, massively! If you want peace and harmony at home, *don't rip the family lawn mower apart, looe some of the bits then try to cover your tracks!*"

"You're really funny!"

"You're really attractive...... "

"Sorry. What did you say?"

"Please don't make me say it again?"

"Why? Don't mess with my head Edward?"

"I...... I think you're...... beautiful-looking, damn it!"

"I don't know what to say. I always thought that you and Pip...... "

"*Pip??* Callum? You and Pip are equally matched when it comes to the love and respect I feel for both of you as friends but...... fuck it, I feel stuff for you that I don't think I should. Things that really confuse me. Stuff happens inside of me when I'm around you. I miss you when you're not with me. You have this knack of making me feel special even though I don't know why, it's sort of a knowing, an inner feeling I have.

Jesus...... I can't even explain it to myself."

Callum fell silent.

I had to say something.

"I've really fucked up big time, haven't I?"

"Yeah...... you have."

"I'm sorry. I'll get my stuff together. I think I'd better leave."

"Leave? Do you know what'll happen if you leave? Let me tell you! You'll be walking away from eighteen of the single most loving and loyal friends you're ever likely to have, and that's just for openers. For the first time that most of those guys can remember, you've shown them that there can be a future off the streets, you're giving them something to cling on to. Why the fuck do you think they're still here? Some of them have been out there since they were like six or seven years old, they know well enough how to fend for themselves, so it isn't me that keeps them here, it's you, shit for brains? They might look upon me as a big brother, I mean, I've been around the block more times than I should've, but when they see you, they see a steady guy, an educated guy, a caring and responsible guy, someone who knows all about the world outside of the back streets.

Buba? That fucking huge West Indian lad? Now, you'd think nothing much would upset him, would you, but when you read to us, I look around, look at the reactions. Do you remember that bit where that girl was attacked by those sharks? Buba cried like an infant, Buba, openly crying? Jesus Christ, Ed? You're able to get past that hard shell they have to have in order to survive, and teach them how to be emotional, and what's more, you're able to show them that it's okay to be like that!"

"I don't want to leave but I've messed up, I've upset you and…… "

"Then don't leave! The only thing, the only person you've upset is you, but…… if you go, not only will you leave a scar on these kid's lives, I'll be devastated as well and I'd most likely pack my bag and follow you."

"Why would you want to do that?"

"For fuck's sake, Ed? Don't you get it? I'm in love with you!"

"You are? Like *really??* "

"Yeah. Like really.

That night I found you camping in my box, you scared the shit out of me. I'd turned a bad trick and I needed to crash big time, but when I saw you, my heart sort of flipped. Don't ask me why 'cos I don't understand it myself.

You stuck around and well…… not only did I not have the heart to tell you to fuck off, I *wanted* you to stay. I liked you, you were different, and okay, I seriously fancied you, I even told you that I wouldn't mind having a boyfriend, but not just *any old* boyfriend? I was trying to send out a message to you that actually, it was *you I wanted* but when you didn't take the hint, I sort of gave up on the idea, but at night I dream that I'm walking down the street with you, hand in hand. You kiss me and it gives me the shivers, but then I wake and it's all over, and that's when I cry.

This isn't about ripping your clothes off and having sex with you, Ed? Oh God, it's so very much more than that. I get lonely, but I've *never* felt the urge to have anyone else share my life…… well ,that is before you trespassed on my property! That was a joke, by the way!

Here was someone, someone dead gorgeous that talked to me like a real human being, someone who was great to be around, made me laugh…… sometimes made me cry, but mostly treated me like I wasn't something nasty they'd picked up on the bottom of their shoe.

Can you have any idea how good that made me feel?

I told you how I got my money and, OH. MY. GOD! You should've seen the look on your face!

It was obvious that you thought I was disgusting, so to stand any chance with you, I gave up the rent because I wanted you to be proud of me.

Please, please don't go?"

Chapter Seven.

T HUMP THUMP, bump-bump-bump, THUMP, bump-bump, THUMP THUMP, bump-bump, THUMP......

"Fucking-hell, Callum? Is this what it sounded like when you got it to run?"

"Yeah, well, until the sodding thing went ape-shit on me!"

"Yes, well, we figured out why that happened. That sight glass was there as a warning. If the oil level went above the line, you were supposed to drain it off, not fill the fucker up! Poor old engine was being fed a diet of pure engine oil to burn!"

"Ooops! Is it doing what it's supposed to do? I mean it sounds like a heap of crap but at least it's running...... sort of."

"It's trying to. See that meter? It's showing that the voltage is sitting at one hundred and ninety, a bit on the low side and that meter there is telling us that she's kicking out a little over three kVA which would seem about par for the course. Now, if I could but work out how to stop the engine, we could trace the wiring and see where it goes.

Have you ever noticed any wall sockets or bulb holders anywhere?"

"Yep. There's a light fitting right above your head, loads in the room next door and a few wall sockets, and maybe try turning the fuel cock off if you want to kill the motor!"

"Oh, yeah! Do we have any bulbs?"

"Are you having a laugh?"

"Okay. More expense then."

"Yeah, but not that much? A pack of batteries cost over three quid, how much is a bulb?"

"I dunno, but we'll need at least two. One for out here and one next door."

"Getting to the light fittings in there'll be a bitch. They're really high up and we don't have a step ladder."

"Okay. We'll take a hike to the recycling place and see if we can't pick up an old table lamp or something."

"Or get one of the boys to knock off a new one?"

"*NO!* This is a one off expense. If we can't find a freebee then we'll fucking-well buy one!"

I thought for a moment.

"There is one other option? I could go back to Solihull and fetch one back from home?"

"Could do I suppose, but considering the cost of train fares, it's probably cheaper to buy one locally."

"Hadn't thought of that. It might be something to think about for the future though? We could make a list of things we could use and if they're back at home, it would make the trip cost-effective. I reckon my mother owes me massively, so I don't have a problem with taking stuff from the house.

Anyway, I'm going down to the pound shop and get us a couple of light bulbs, fancy walking with me?"

*****

It was Saturday, and with no need for precautions, Callum and I squeezed through the hole in the wall and out into the alley.

One of the things with him was, around me he was never lost for conversation and as we walked, he was babbling on about nothing in particular so remembering something, I shut him up.

"Shhh! Wait up a bit!"

"What's up? Anything the matter?"

"Not exactly the matter, but something could be better."

"Such as?"

"Such as this!"

I leaned across and took his hand in mine, and smiling into his rather shocked eyes said, "Come on then? We've got light bulbs to buy!"

Callum tried unsuccessfully to pull his hand away. "But…… Ed, we can't be seen like this!"

"Why not? What's so wrong about us holding hands?"

"It's gay, that's what's wrong!"

"So…… you're straight all of a sudden then?"

"Em, no? But what about you!"

"Let me think for a moment.

Got it!

I'm holding the hand of the most beautiful person that has ever entered my life, and not only that, I couldn't give a fuck what people wanna make of it."

"Oh God."

"Oh God what?"

"I think I'm going to cry!"

"For fuck's sake don't do that or you'll have Pip racing around the corner accusing me of molesting you!"

"Hahahaha!! Thank you, Mr Edward Anderson! Situation defused!"

"You're welcome, Mr Callum Lee!"

*****

The Pound shop provided us with what we needed and then some. Low energy bulbs, a cheapo table lamp, a pack of batteries and a pair of thick rubber gloves, and all for a fiver.

We ambled back, not bothering taking to the side streets but rather taking the opportunity to window-shop, all the time holding hands, and wanna know something?

No one so much as gave us a second glance!

We walked further up the street than we usually did, stopping off to buy a bag of sherbet pips from an Indian sweet shop before finding the far entrance to our alley, and it was here I wanted to make Callum's dream a reality.

As was his habit, he was rabbiting on nineteen to the dozen, obviously happy as he had his fingers intertwined with mine and swinging our arms forward and back in time with our footsteps.

I made my move and spinning him around and with all the finesse of a sexed up rhino, I leaned into him and found his lips with mine.

Okay...... very Barbara Cartland, but I think my world stopped turning momentarily. I felt clumsy and awkward yet completely and utterly at ease with what I was doing.

Callum stiffened up then relaxed into me returning my kiss.

We eventually separated, our eyes misted over. We held hands and cuddled, that was until we heard someone clear their throat.

"And about time too!"

We both spun around to see Pip smiling at us.

"Sorry, but if you don't want to be seen, then may I suggest you find somewhere a little less public?"

Callum was caught completely on the back foot.

"Pip...... "

"Pip what! Didn't you hear me? I said, and I quote, about time too! You guys have been mooning over each other since like, forever! It was inevitable, written in the stars or whatever! I'm very happy for both of you as will the others once you tell them! Anyway, let's get home 'cos I've got a surprise for you"

*****

Pip was animated!

"My best scam ever and I didn't even have to lie, although I did say that the engine was called a Bollinger!"

"Oh right. The Champagne of heavy oil engines then!"

"Shut it, Ed! Anyway, someone I know works for Brocks, you know, the firework people? So, anyhow, I told him about our genny and the need for something to warm the fuel. I was thinking that maybe some of that paper stuff you set a match at that sort of fizzes before a firework goes off might do, but he had a better idea, a slow-burn fuse like the ones they use for big display jobbies. Half an inch will smoulder for like twenty seconds, he reckons, so he managed to get hold of about twelve inches of the stuff."

"Sounds as if it might work, but to prove the point, we'll have to let the engine cool right down first. For now, we can fit the bulbs, and later when the engines running, we can swing the isolator, check to make sure the wiring doesn't catch fire then see if we've got lighting."

Callum took the bulbs out of the bag and fitted one to the table lamp and the other to the overhead light socket before pulling out the rubber gloves.

"I meant to ask you at the time, but why did you get these?"

"Insulate myself. If I swing the isolator only to find that somethings shorted out inside, it'll send me flying, so they'll stop that from happening."

"All of a sudden I don't feel so confident! First you tell me the place might go up in a cloud of smoke, and second, you might kill yourself. Do we really wanna do this?"

"Yes, sure we do! Everything ought to be fine. The wiring is fairly modern twin and earth and the isolator looks to be alright, I mean, if I had a screwdriver, I could open it up and take a look, but as I haven't, we'll just have to trust to luck and a pair of Marigolds."

"How come you know about all this stuff, Ed?"

"I read a lot, plus we were taught the basics at school, but that doesn't make me an expert, just very conscious of safety I suppose."

Pip stood up and stretched. "I'm going into town and take a look around that market. Want to join me?"

Callum grabbed his coat. "Yeah, sounds like a plan? How about you, Ed?"

"Um, no I don't think so. I want to go through this manual again, so if it's all the same to you, I think I'll stay here."

"Yeah, okay. We won't be gone that long."

"Don't worry, Ed, I'll keep your boyfriend out of mischief!"

"Pip? Please don't take the piss? I never said he was my boyfriend?"

"Whatever. Laterz, Ed."

"Yeah, laterz, guys."

*****

Half an hour later and finding it difficult to concentrate on the instruction manual, found me sipping coffee at Ronny's.

It was quiet, no taxis parked up in the street, and no other customers so Ronny and I fell into conversation.

"You look a bit down in the dumps, Ed? Is everything alright?"

"Yes and no. Yes, in as much as we've found this old generator and surprise, surprise, we managed to get it running, but no, 'cos I feel very guilty over summat."

"Do you wanna talk about it?"

"The generator or my guilt?"

"Both if you want, but as this generator sounds like good news, why not tackle what's eating at you first."

"Not much to say to be honest. I said something hurtful to Callum and now I feel really bad about it. I wasn't totally honest with him and he deserved better."

"So, you lied to him, is that it?"

"No...... I didn't exactly *lie* to him, I was caught on the hop and didn't have time to think of a proper response, and so what I came out with, I dunno, cut him to the quick I guess."

"You like him a lot, huh?"

"Yeah, yeah, I do."

"So, where is he now?"

"Gone to the German market with Pip."

"Okay? So now's your chance to think of that proper response, and when he gets back, put it to him and apologise for being thoughtless. If he's a true friend, he'll forgive you."

"Thanks Ronny."

"No worries. So what's with this generator then?"

"We found this genny, well Callum found it really. It's old like ancient-type old, definitely pre-war, and between us we got it to run so with a bit of luck we can use it to give us a bit of light."

"Petrol or diesel?"

"Neither. It's a heavy oil motor, whatever that's supposed to mean. We're using diesel at the present but Callum had it running on engine oil the one time."

"I've heard about them. They'll run on just about any flammable fuel oil so whatever you do, don't go nicking diesel 'cos I can give you as much oil as you can use."

"Wow! I mean thanks, but how come?"

"Got a deep fat fryer and the oil has to be changed every three or four days. Some bloke comes and takes the old stuff away for recycling into biofuel but I get nothing from him, so you're welcome to take as much as you like. You'll have to filter it to get shot of any solids like bits of batter and the like, an old pair of ladies tights are good for doing that, otherwise you just chuck it in and job's a good-un."

"Ronny? You're a mate!"

"Forget it, Ed. Honestly, you're very welcome.

Now, have you decided what you're going to say to Callum?"

*****

"So, shall we go see if this taper caper works then?"

"Yes, if you want."

"I want, but you don't seem too keen? It could be the answer to our prayers?"

"Sorry. Okay let's do it, and if it works and if the electric's okay, I wanna talk to you. Well, I wanna talk to you anyway, but first things first, yeah?"

"Whatever."

*****

THUMP, bump, bump, THUMP THUMP, bump, bump, bump...... THUMP, bump, bump......

"Fucking-hell. Second bloody kick! You gonna try the electrics?"

"Yep. Pass me those gloves will you?"

"Yeah and then I'm going to stand well back. I don't like messing with stuff I don't understand."

"It's me doing the messing, so stop being such a wimp! Just keep an eye on that volt meter and tell me if it dips."

I took a deep breath and briefly wondering if it might be my last, tuned the isolator to its 'ON' position. No blinding flash, no smoke so far as I could tell, so I shouted down the passageway to Callum.

"Anything?"

"What do you mean by anything? Nothing happened!"

"The volt meter never moved then?"

"Nah, not even a twitch.

Hang on a mo...... yeah, somethings happened. The light's come on!"

"What? All by itself like on?"

"Don't be a dick? I turned the fucker on!"

"Pfff! Thank God for that! Let's go see if the wall sockets are okay."

There were four in total, two on each wall, and having sniffed at them, then touching them in case they were getting hot, I crossed fingers and toes and turned on the table lamp.

"YES!!!!! WE HAVE LIFT-OFF!!!!"

I sat down beside the lamp, picked up our current storybook and flicked through the pages.

More than good enough!

Callum came running over and high-fived me.

"What a fucking RESULT!"

"Pretty damn awesome! Let's leave the genny to run 'cos we need to talk."

"Yeah, okay."

"But not here, let's go into next doors yard 'cos what I want to say is private."

"Lead on then."

*****

"I was horrible to you earlier and I want to say sorry."

"When was that?"

"Don't be a twatt all your life? When Pip said he'd keep you out of mischief."

"So, I remember that but how were you horrible?"

"He referred to you as my boyfriend and I put him down, put *you* down."

"Yeah, well, Pip sometimes opens his mouth before putting his brain in gear. I wouldn't worry about it."

"But *I do* worry about it, damn it? Will you promise you'll just listen to me for a moment?"

"Sure, but...... "

"Callum?"

"Sorry."

"Look, he implied that we were an item and I denied it!"

"No, you didn't? You never said I was your boyfriend and you haven't, so where's your problem, Ed?"

"My problem is...... I wanted to but I couldn't! You said you were in love with me, I took the initiative and held your hand, I even kissed you, so *why can't I just cut the bullshit and admit it? You're the most amazing, lovely, beautiful person I've ever known and I WANT THE WORLD TO KNOW!!"*

Oh God, oh God! Callum stepped forward, and putting one arm around my waste and his other hand on the back of my head, pulled me into him and kissed me deeply. We opened up to each other and kissed and kissed until I thought I'd cum in my pants, but then he pulled away slightly and giggled.

"And if you go shouting it out fit to wake the dead, then it won't just be the whole world in the loop, it'll be the entire fucking universe!

Come on *boyfriend!* Let's go spread the word around, shall we?"

Chapter Eight.

I later told Pip and Callum about Ronny's offer of giving us some spent cooking oil, so before he handed over for the day, we paid him a visit.

Callum and I borrowed Ronny's sack barrow and carted fifty litres back home while Pip went to buy a pair of tights. I think he drew the shorter of the two straws as he returned red-faced with embarrassment!

"What a nerve! Did I want black, barely black, tan, skin, satin, shiny, what size was I, what denier did I want?

Oh, for heaven's sake!"

Both Callum and I creased up! "So, what did you go for, sweet thing?? I reckon tan, shiny and ten denier would look good on those legs. What do you think, Ed?"

"I'm with you on the tan, but wouldn't you think satin might show off those sexy calf muscles better?"

"Nah. But if he was to go for barely black? Oh yeah! With you one hundred percent!"

"Alright, ALL-FUCKING-RIGHT ALREADY!

Yeah, okay I'll go with the funny but can it why don't you!"

*****

We played the waiting game until Buba came back.

Buba is one seriously big boy, not fat but built like brick shit-house and we needed his muscle power to help lift the oil drums so we could filter it into the fuel tank.

Unfortunately, Callum was still on a high.

"So, is it true what they say, Buba?"

"What's that, man?"

"All you black guys are like, hung?"

"Nah. Us dudes is normal jumbo hotdogs. It's you white trash who haven't so much as a cocktail sausage to call your own!!"

That was it. Buba was shaking so hard with a fit of the giggles that tank-filling had to be put on ice until we'd all calmed down!

By the time we'd filled it as much as we dared, it was getting dark so we restarted the engine and went through to the big room for the evening.

Tonight, with the slow, erratic thumping of the engine, the glow from the table lamp and our fire taking the edge off the chill, everything was well with my world.

I read until I noticed eyes getting heavy, went through and shut the engine down for the night then crawled into our sleeping bag.

Callum smiled at me. Yes, he was smiling, not grinning. His jet black eyes radiated love, a tenderness I'd not seen before from him or from anybody else come to that.

He held open his arms and I fell into them.

Holding me close and with my head resting on his chest, he spoke softly to me.

"Are you okay, Ed? It's been something of a day, hasn't it."

"You could say that. One moment everything is alright, the next? Something happens to spoil it, but then the Gods rain down on us and I honestly believe that right now, right at this minute, life could not be better."

"You're sharing a sleeping bag with someone who is technically an illegal immigrant, you're surrounded by difficult and challenged kids, you live in a hovel with almost no money, surviving each day with little hope of a decent future and you say life couldn't be better?"

"I mean it Callum. Let's turn that on its head shall we?

I know your story and okay, you were brought into this country illegally but you were only like what, two years old? You can't possibly be held to account over something your surrogate parents did? I think that deporting them was cruel. They did what they did because they had no other options open to them.

I know some of these guys have issues but then so do I, so do you, but let me ask you something. When was the last time you saw any signs of conflict or nastiness? I haven't seen any, and I'll bet you haven't either. We're all in this together, as individuals we're weak, but together? We will get through it, and whether they're conscious of it or not, they recognise that deep down.

This place? It might be that one day they'll redevelop the area and we'll have to leave, but for now, it's ours. Let's not think too much about the future, it'll be what it'll be and nothing we do can stop it from happening. We must live our lives for the here and now, and right now, right this minute, if I owned a penthouse in Manhattan or a beach villa in the Caribbean, I'd trade everything to be here with you."

Callum buried his head in my chest and wept silently. I made no attempt to stop him.

Eventually we drifted off to sleep but not before I kissed each of his fingers.

Tomorrow? Another day and more challenges, but just for now...... I was happy.

*****

"You awake Ed?"

"Just about. What's the time?"

"According to the church clock, a little after nine."

"Oh. We ought to think about getting up then."

"Can we just stay like this for a while please?"

"I'd stay like this all day given the chance! Yesterday was wonderful and a new day might spoil things."

"Ever thought that a new day could be even better than an old one?"

"Not possible. I don't believe that anything could ever come close. We managed to get the genny running, we were offered an almost limitless supply of fuel for it, we've got light, Ronny helped me to get things straight in my head and I finally plucked up the courage to tell you what I should've told you ages ago."

"Yeah, okay, it was pretty special. Will you kiss me Ed?"

"Only if you can handle a touch of morning breath, I forgot to clean my teeth last night!"

"I can do that. Please, Ed?"

*****

Sunday meant tidying up day. It was easy to let the place get mucky what with there being nineteen of us living there, so it was agreed that we would all pitch in and do our bit to stay on top of things.

We had an old watering can which we'd fill from the canal then sprinkle the water onto the floor to lay the dust then sweep it into a pile and shovel it out into the alley.

Boxes had to either be repaired or replaced, so trips to the recycling centre were made, and it was this Sunday that two of the lads returned with something more than what they'd originally planned on scrounging. A set of Christmas lights.

"This bloke was about to chuck 'em so I asked if he would give 'em to us. He reckoned four of the bulbs were fucked and he'd bought a new set...... some people have more money than sense if you ask me!"

I thought about this for a moment.

"What we need is a tree to string them up in."

Tiny laughed.

"Nice one, Ed, but if you hadn't noticed, the Digbeth district of Birmingham ain't exactly awash with Christmas trees going begging!"

"Maybe, maybe not! I'm going out 'cos I'm feeling lucky!"

Back to the recycling centre and casting my eyes around, I concentrated on the skip marked Non-recyclable Waste and waited patiently. A few cars came and went before I stuck paydirt.

A family piled out of a large SUV and proceeded to offload the usual junk before one rather large artificial Christmas tree got pulled from the back of the vehicle.

I approached the kid who was struggling with it.

"Wow! Nice tree! Why are you chucking it away?"

"My brother stood on the base and broke it. No base? No point in hanging on to it. Do you want it?"

"Well, yeah, I do actually. We haven't got a Christmas tree and can't afford to buy one, so if you're offering?"

"Hang on, I'll ask my Dad.

Dad? Is it okay if this boy has our old tree?"

"If he can use it then fine, give it to him."

The kid grinned at me. "Looks as if you've just blagged yourself a tree! Here y'go and Happy Chrimbo!"

"And to you, mate. Cheers!"

*****

Blagging it was easy enough, getting it home was another matter...... the sodding thing was HUGE! It had to be at least six-foot long, and with no string to keep the branches tied back meant I kept tripping over them, but non-the-less, I persevered finally making it back without doing much damage to either myself or the bloody tree!

With some help from Pip, we managed to get it through the hole in the wall then set about the task of rearranging the branches so it looked like the real deal.

No cheap artificial tree this. No, this was seriously up-market stuff and must have cost an arm and a leg, but now came the problem of how to support it.

We eventually settled on cutting the top off an old water bowser from next door's yard, then with a couple of the boys holding on to the tree to keep it upright, we packed the bowser with a mixture of lumps of concrete and clay dug from the canal bank, then once satisfied our tree wasn't about to fall over, we stood back and admired our handiwork.

Impressive came to mind!

Next, we tested the lights.

Four of them refused to light, but that was okay as these were outdoor lamps and came in a length of what I estimated to be around fifty feet, so more than enough to decorate our six-footer. It looked really nice, but then Callum spoke up.

"It does look nice but there's something missing."

Pip giggled. "If it needs a fairy to sit on top of it, you'd better figure out a way to get yourself up there!"

Callum poked his tongue out at him and laughed. "Yeah, okay, funny fucker! No, what it needs is something for the lamps to reflect off. Any ideas people?"

Silence, then one of the younger lads put up his hand.

"CD's. You know, like used data discs. I saw it in a park once, someone had strung a load of them up in a tree and when the wind spun 'em around, the light that hit 'em looked just like rainbows."

"Fucking ace idea Parker, fu-cking A!

One small problem.

We don't have any."

"Why not go back to the dump?"

"Okay? Your idea, you go, and if you find some, I'll give you half a bag of sherbet pips!"

"Deal!

I'm gone!"

As Parks disappeared through the hole in the wall, I turned to Callum. "Know summat? You might just regret doing that deal?"

"Oh, I do hope so. I *really do hope so!*"

*****

With Callum now light of half a bag of sherbet pips, a crowd of us sat outside and began cutting the discs into four like little fans then using pen knives we gouged a hole in the pointed part and poked string through them and tied them off. More kids came out, and taking them away, got on with the job of hanging them up.

The upper-most branches presented a problem but one of the more enterprising lads had his mate sit on his shoulders, and after about half an hour it was finished.

We probably had one more hour of daylight left to us, so with no real need to waste fuel by running the genny, we didn't take a look at the finished article, preferring to wait until later, but then Mitch came up with an idea.

"As things stand, and with most of the guys out and about, they've not even seen the tree, let alone with it all lit up and decorated, so I wondered. Tomorrow is Christmas Eve, so why not leave it until it gets dark tomorrow evening before switching it on. You can pretty much bet that most, if not all of us will be here, and it would make for a really nice Christmas surprise. What do you reckon?"

Pip looked at Callum and me. "What do you think? Personally, I think Mitch's idea's really good. Let's be honest, Christmas is normally a fuck-nothing day. Nowhere's open, not even Ronny's place, we've sod-all to celebrate except for Bobby who goes to church, so why not keep the tree as something special?"

I nodded my head.

"Works for me," then turning to Callum, "What say you then?"

"Yep. I like that idea muchly!"

Pip continued.

"All sorted, but there's just one other thing, although I think it might be nice if we keep it to ourselves for now.

Tomorrow late afternoon, I plan on hitting on Tesco to see what stuff they'll have to throw out, and if I get lucky, I might be able to scrounge a few goodies for Christmas Day. Want to come along for the ride?"

"We're in…… aren't we, Ed!"

"Bring it on!"

"Thought you might be! Come on, let's get ourselves down to Ronny's 'cos I wanna get back and find out if, <giggle>, Callum Lee, super hero and all-round gay super-stud, manages to escape from the clutches of that totally insane and crazy I.S. terror group! Love ya to bits really…… Mr S.A.S!!"

*****

He did escape…… well he was always going to, wasn't he!

The kids loved it as well, and so with book finished, I wondered what to go for next.

It had to fire their imagination, but then I wanted to read something to them that made them feel good inside at the end of each chapter…… I call it the 'thank fuck for that' syndrome, not the fuzzy 'Oh, isn't that nice' thing of trashy novels, but what?

I decided on pure comedy and Tom Sharpe.

I've always loved the stuff he wrote, it was pure escapism, work that could always take me into a place where I could laugh no matter how much my life stank. I must've read Porterhouse Blue a hundred times...... well, maybe not *really* a hundred times, but you take my point.

No, this was what I was going to go for next, but for now my thoughts seemed to prefer to dwell on Christmas' past when my parents and I were a cohesive and normal middle class suburban family, those times before the bickering turned into furious arguments, those times before my father stormed out of the house and out of my life, those times before my mother's steep decline into drugs and alcohol, and I wondered why I wasn't upset, but then, looking to my left, I knew why. I was looking at a beautiful if potty-mouthed Vietnamese boy, a boy who had openly declared his love for me and me for him.

I removed my socks, and slipping into our sleeping bag, I kissed him on the cheek.

"Sweet dreams Callum. I love you."

He muttered something, then putting his free arm around me, I drifted off to sleep.

Chapter Nine.

"I 'm going out this morning, stuff I need to do, so if there's nothing you need me for, I'll get off."

"Want me to come with you, Ed?"

"No, but thanks anyway, this is something I want to do by myself."

"Okay but keep your phone with you."

"Yeah, I've got it. Shouldn't be that long, I'll probably be back by around lunchtime."

"Are you sure you don't want me to tag along? If it's like private stuff, I won't go asking questions?"

"Look, Callum? I need to get back to Solihull, there's stuff there I need, and yes, okay I'd love you to come with me, but I've only got enough money for my rail fare."

"Then I'm deffo coming with you. Safety in numbers, remember? And anyway, I've got enough cash to cover my own costs. Let me go grab my coat and I'll go and tell Pip where we're going just in case of trouble."

*****

It was Christmas Eve and all the last-minute shoppers meant the city centre was fast becoming busy, but as we were heading out of town rather than into town, our train was almost empty and we could sit for the entire journey.

I had wondered about being recognised, but then my hair had grown out considerably, and with a beanie pulled down almost obscuring my vision, I was as well disguised as I could be, and anyway, what did it matter if I was?

I did notice a couple of kids from my old school waiting at Solihull station, but they didn't appear to notice me, making the walk back to the house uneventful.

We crouched park side of the fence at the bottom of the garden and checked for movement at both my next-door neighbour's houses, but all was quiet and with both sets of curtains drawn, I guessed both families were away for the duration so we scooted through the garden to the back door and let ourselves in.

"I know you said it was sort of a private trip, but what exactly *did* you come back for?"

"Presents for the kids mainly. Up in the attic there are loads of old games and stuff, all perfectly okay and probably not best suited to our lot given their ages, but then I got to thinking. When you've got nothing, to have at least something *has* to be a bonus, it's kicking about and it's free, so why not?"

"Yeah, well, I'm sure they'll appreciate it. Lead the way then!"

*****

Passing what I thought were the most suitable items down to Callum, he packed them into suitcases before we took a break for coffee.

"That case is pretty much full. Is there much more up there?"

"No more games, but there's boxes of my old clothes that are too small for me, so I thought we'd take some of the better things, and if any of the kids want them, they can have them."

"Jesus, Ed? You'd never have managed to get this lot back by yourself? Fucking good job I came with you!"

"Yeah, and actually, I wish now I'd asked Pip as well 'cos I'm not done yet."

"I'll give him a shout, shall I? He could be here in about half an hour?"

"Yes, okay. Do it, but tell him to put his skates on, we've still got that Tesco thing to do later on."

*****

We finished packing and while Callum was busy brewing more coffee and waiting for Pip to show up, I went to see if I could find the one thing I had really come for.

I had wanted to buy something special for Callum, but with cash not exactly being my biggest asset, I decided to take something from home. Fortunately, I managed to find what I was looking for with relative ease, so stuffing it in my pocket, I took one more look around my mother's bedroom before being drawn to her wardrobe and an overwhelming urge to look inside took hold.

Dresses, blouses, skirts and shoes. Loads of bloody shoes, and as the majority of this gear was bought while my folks were still together, I can only imagine that much of this stuff was on the high end in a scale of one to ten in the quality stakes, and the thought crossed my mind, 'Ebay it!', but no way of getting on line meant that was a non-starter.

I went to close the door when a shoe fell off the top shelf and clouted me on the forehead.

"Ouch! Shit!"

I stuffed it back from whence it came which caused two more to fall to the floor, but this time I left them there and again I went to close the door, but then I saw something else, something I'd thought I'd lost for ever.

It was my old cashbox.

I grabbed it and gave it a shake. No rattle of coins but there was definitely something inside, so I ran to the top of the stairs and shouted for Callum.

"Here, catch this and I'll be down in a minute!"

I closed up, and taking one more look around, I chased down the stairs just as Pip wandered in.

"What-ho guys! Is that coffee I smell?"

He then took a look around the kitchen, and seeing the cases said,

"Jesus, you blokes, what on earth is in those cases!"

"Later. First I need to open this sodding box!"

I found my keys and fingered through them before finding the right one, and with my hands trembling with anticipation, I unlocked the box and threw open the lid.

Vocal as always, Callum was the first to speak. "Fucking-hell, Ed? How much dosh is *in there?"*

"God knows, a lot by the looks of things! Let's count it."

*****

"Eleven sixty, eleven eighty, twelve hundred. Twelve hundred quid!!! Exactly the amount that arsehole nicked from my bank account!

Come on, let's get out of here!"

We left by the front door with three large, heavy cases, three table lamps, a supply of bulbs and my pockets stuffed with twenty pound notes.

A well productive morning!

We got to the station just as our train pulled in, and once we were seated, Pip asked the inevitable question.

"If he nicked your money, why didn't he spend it?"

"Search me. Maybe it wasn't him after all, maybe it was my mother who took it, hid it from him so keeping it somewhere safe for me.

Maybe I've misjudged her, who knows but at least I've got it back."

"What do you plan on doing with it? Bank it or spend it?"

"First off, bank it. I can get to one of those credit point machines before we hit Tesco's and then I can get shot of it, change my access code then think about stuff, but what I might well do is buy a serviceable laptop so I can get online."

"Yeah but why the need to get online, Ed?"

"You've both seen my house? It's banged full of stuff, quality stuff I'll never use, so I intend to flog it, make some money off the back of it.

I reckon I'm owed."

"Flog it from where though? Can't hardly do it from our place?"

"Do it from the house. Stick the stuff on auction and if we get any takers, which we will, then we go back to Solihull and do the business there. Problem sorted!"

"We?"

"Yes, *we*! I'll tell you something else. I'll be giving both of you my new access code 'cos if anything happens to me, I want both of you to be able to get your mitts on my money."

"Do you trust us enough, Ed? I mean we could always do a runner!"

"Sure, you could, but I know you too well. I love Callum, he loves me and you, Pip, are my best mate, so?"

"Okay! You're right of course, of course we wouldn't go touching it, but do you wanna know what is touching? Your faith in us, that's what!"

*****

Our luck held good at Tesco's.

Callum was all for stealing stuff out of the bins but I had a different idea, and once I'd managed to get Pip onside, we made our way through front entrance of the store to the Customer Service desk and asked if we could speak to the store manager.

He met us but I don't think he was best impressed.

"So, what do you lot want?"

"I was going to say a sympathetic ear, but that isn't right because that's a step too far. What we're hoping for is your permission to help ourselves to some perishables that would otherwise go to waste."

"What makes you think that there will be any? Our stock control means that we minimise wastage."

"I know that you try your best, but then neither do you want to run short of anything as that wouldn't show off your brand very well. Everyone understands there has to be a degree of wastage and all we're asking for is to be allowed to take some of it."

"Why did you come to me? Most people just steal it."

"Try, we want to be honest? We're street children, we don't have much money, but then neither are we bad people. Sure, we nick stuff when we have no other choice, and okay, rough we may be, but our hearts are in the right place."

"You, young man, sound as if you've received an education. Odd for a street kid, wouldn't you say?"

"Hatton Grammar School, that is until my family disintegrated."

"What house were you in?"

"Leamington."

"What is so special about Warwick House?"

"Nothing. They're a bunch of idiots, their heads planted so far up their arses that they think they're a cut above the rest."

"Right answer. I was in Stratford when I was there!

Go out the way you came and I'll get someone to meet you at the rear of the store in a few minutes."

*****

Three trolley loads later, and said trollies returned to the store, we took an inventory of everything we'd been given.

Turkey breasts aplenty, stuffing balls, vegetables, stock cubes, potatoes, a number of damaged Christmas puddings, tins of soup (bent of course), Sausages, bacon, eggs, bread, butter, three cases of Coca-Cola and two of lemonade, milk by the gallon, biscuits, cheese and three huge tins of sweets.

"Fucking-hell. Where are we going to keep this stuff!"

"Get as much of the meat as you can into the fridge together with the cheese and butter. The milk we can dunk in the canal, that'll keep it cool enough and the containers are tough enough to stop the rats from getting to it. Put all the cans of drink by the Christmas tree together with the sweets, I dunno what we do with the bread, I'll think of summat later, the rest can live in the cupboard as it seems rat-free."

"Yeah but I'm worried about the fucking bread, Ed?"

"Alright. Empty the smaller of the suitcases, find somewhere to plug in the table lamps, shove the spare bulbs in the cupboard and what clothing there is, we sleep on top of, the bread can live in the suitcase for now."

"Plan! Do you want me to fire up the genny?"

"Yes, please Callum, but let's not light the tree until everyone's back."

*****

I think it was gone seven in the evening before everyone was home. The conversation was the usual talk of the day's activities like scamming this and thieving that, but no one seemed in anyway excited by the fact that it was Christmas Eve, in fact the opposite was the case. Miserable faces, down-beat over the prospect that nowhere would be open so no point in getting out of bed come the morning.

I voiced my feelings in a chat with Pip and Callum who didn't appear to share my concerns.

"What you've got to remember is, none of them can probably remember a Christmas where they felt secure. They live from hand to mouth and Christmas is the one time of the year there isn't a hand to feed the mouth."

"I hear you, but I just know there's going to be this attitude of 'so what the fuck' when we turn on the lights, all that effort for what? Disinterest? All those grand illuminations all around the city and then ours? A pathetic attempt to get into the spirit of things. I've got this horrible feeling it's going to fall flat on its face."

"Bollocks! Have some faith, Ed!

I'm fed up of waiting so I'm going to take it upon myself and announce the tree ceremony so get over there and be ready to switch the lights on when I say"

*****

"Listen up people! Who can tell me what day it is today?"

One lone voice in amongst the mutterings.

"Christmas-fucking-Eve. So what!"

"Yeah…… Christmas-fucking-Eve, but what if things could be better?"

Another voice spoke up.

"It sort of already is. At least we're all together, but Christmas is still so much shit."

"Yeah, we're all together and if that wasn't special enough? Hit the lights, Ed!"

The tree lit up, and with the little CD fans reflecting their rainbows around the room, the place fell silent. Seriously, you could've heard a pin drop, and after what seemed like forever, Bobby got to his feet and began to sing.

'Silent night, holy night
All is calm, all is bright.
'Round yon virgin Mother and child.
Holy infant so tender and mild.
Sleep in heavenly peace…
Sleep in heavenly peace.'

Bobby's pitch-perfect soprano voice echoed around the room, and just as soon as he'd finished, another voice began to sing the same verse, and slowly the entire room was singing.

Twice this happened then a round of applause and the room settled down.

I wiped the tears from my eyes, and to break the impasse, stood up and made my own announcement.

"Holy shit Bobby? I don't think I've ever felt so moved, not ever. Thank you for bringing a little bit of the spirit of Christmas into this place."

"No worries Ed. I know that I'm probably the only one here who believes, but try to look at it like this. That kid Jesus was born to unmarried parents. Not a good start! They were poor, and he was born in a barn surrounded by animals far away from home, and yet he went on to be the saviour of all mankind. He got himself murdered, but before that happened, he did things, good things that made a difference, and the way I see it, if he can do it, so can we. I mean we ain't so different from him, are we? We're poor, we live in a barn…… sort of, so think about it."

"Cheers Bobby. Well spoken, and while we on the subject of being poor? Tonight, we're rich! Under the tree you'll find cans of pop and tins of sweets, so go help yourselves, BUT, a word of caution. Don't go getting greedy! This lot has to last us tonight and tomorrow and Boxing Day, and if I find ANYONE hording stuff, I'll fucking slay them. Take what you need, and if you want to come back for more later on then fine, but please be considerate, okay?"

Tiny was quick-witted and no mistake!

"I take you mean slay as in kill, not sleigh as in Father Christmas? If that old bastard tried to come down our chimney, he'd fry his arse!"

"Funny fucker!

On the subject of food, we have enough gear to do a passable job on tomorrow's Christmas lunch, but we'll need your help.

It makes no odds if you're crap at cooking, washing up and preparing stuff is just as important, so it'd be good if everyone could lend a hand."

I handed over to Callum.

"You heard the man? Ed has a new book, so go and grab yourself something and we can get settled down for the evening and…… Happy Christmas!"

Chapter Ten.

I t was my turn to tend the fire that night, and that plus the un-seasonably mild weather had me sweating, so throwing cau-tion to the wind, I slipped out of my jumper and shirt and re-moved my jeans. I settled into our sleeping bag, and with Callum snoring gently, fell to sleep almost as soon as I lay down, not waking until I felt a hand running up my back underneath my vest.

"I'm sorry Ed but I've never seen you like this before, shower-ing aside, and I needed to touch you like, properly and Oh My God, do you feel good!"

His gentle hands caressing me sent shivers running up and down my spine, and no matter what he did next would've bothered me, but he left it at that, just held me close and cuddled me.

I drifted back to sleep, not waking until I heard the generator fire up.

I allowed myself time to come to terms with the fact that an-other day had dawned, but then looking at the tree and realising it was Christmas Day, I rolled out of our sleeping bags and went to retrieve my jeans.

Tiny saw me and joked,

"You look like you had some fun last night?"

"Sod you. It was warm, too warm for keeping these on."

"Hot more like! Don't let it bother you, Ed! Anyway, I smell coffee, you coming?"

111

I followed him out. Most of the boys were already outside sitting cross-legged on the ground, mugs in hand and talking, so Tiny and I found a space, and helping ourselves to coffee, settled in to a conversation of our own.

"There's some sort of an event going on. Fucking loads of boats on the move. What do you reckon it is?"

"Like I'm an expert! Why don't you ask Callum?"

"I did but I didn't get his answer."

"What was that?"

"BCN Challenge or summat. Held every year or so he said. I still don't have a clue what he's on about!"

"Nor me. Wanna go find out?"

"Yeah, why not! I'll just go and find Callum and tell him where we plan on going just in case he needs a hand getting stuff ready for lunch."

"Don't bother. He's saved you the trouble as it looks as if he's going out somewhere as well."

He trotted over to where we were sitting.

"I'm talking a stroll down to Farmers Bridge Top Lock and watch some of the boats go through. Fancy joining me? We might even make us some money in the process.

Here, grab these."

Callum held out two windlass's which Tiny and I took but questioned why.

"I'll explain while we walk."

*****

"The BCN Challenge is held every year and lasts for twenty-four hours. The idea is that you have boats with crews that try to cover as many of the canals around Birmingham as possible, doing as many locks as they can and the one who has the highest score is the winner.

To make the most of it, these boats have at least four on board, sometimes six, so as one crew sleeps, the other is driving the boat then after twelve hours they swap over. If we help them through the lock, it makes it quicker for them so they stand a better chance of winning. Last year, me and Pip made almost sixty quid. Not bad for three hours graft!"

"Sixty quid is only like, ten quid an hour?"

"Sixty quid *each* Ed but we sort of cheated! We latched on to just the one boat and took them up through the complete Farmers Bridge Flight so every lock was all ready and waiting for them. We took a break then did it all over again for another boat and both skippers gave us fifty and that plus a couple more boats at the top lock netted us sixty each!"

"Shit! Shame this challenge is only once a year!"

"Yeah, but come the summer, that canal gets busy as it's like a short cut down to Coventry. Hit onto a boat that belongs to old gits or maybe just someone on their own and do the same, saving them the arse-ache of getting on and off their boat all the time and you can easily make two-hundred in a day, and, because they're in no hurry, you're not busting your balls all day!"

"Now that *is* a nice little earner, but there's one small problem. I don't have a clue how to work locks."

"It's a piece of piss, Ed. If I can do it then it'll be a breeze for you. Let's go make us some money!"

*****

Working as a team of three and after Callum explained how to go about things, we made fast progress for one boat, getting it up the entire flight of thirteen locks in double-quick time which netted us twenty quid each. The method we used was, because the boats were climbing the flight, all three of us got the boat in to the lock through the double gates then once they were shut, I was left to open the paddles and flood it, open the top single gate to let the boat out, lower the paddle, shut the gate whilst Callum and Tiny set the next lock ready for the boat to enter, and so on. They'd set the lock, I'd fill it and let the boat out as they prepared the next one.

Three boats, and each of us richer by sixty pounds, we made our way back, more than ready for our Christmas lunch.

*****

Buba had relished the opportunity to chef for all of us and to his credit, had exceeded all expectations. Clever use of our barbeque, old biscuit tins suspended over open fires as make-shift ovens provided the means to cook the meal of turkey breasts, boiled vegetables, roast potatoes and gravy, but the most ingenious use of resources was saved for the Christmas puddings.

Buba had thought about how these could be steamed. They needed time to heat through and we didn't have a way to keep the temperature constant enough to do the business...... or did we?

We did, and he tied string around the pre-packaged puddings and lowered them into the cooling tank of the generator's engine which had a near-continuous temperature of seventy degrees Celsius.

There were no left-overs to get rid of except old Christmas Cracker paper, not even paper hats as most of us kept them on all day, finally burning them on our fire before turning in for the night which was very late by our reckoning as the games I'd brought from home had gone down a storm.

I must admit that I had been worried that those might be too young for our lot, but even Tiddly-Winks got a good thrashing. Pictionary, Monopoly, Cluedo, just about everything was played and all returned to their respective boxes for use another day.

Most of the sweets were gone except for a tin Pip had kept back for Boxing Day, and we still had enough cans of drink left over, so with that, and the generator silenced, we headed to bed.

*****

I woke early. Very early, and despite feeling knackered, I got dressed and went outside to brew some coffee but I forgot that the genny wasn't running so no juice for the electric kettle.

I went back inside and kicked it over, not caring if it woke anyone. I needed coffee.

I sat by the canal and watched the many boats that were still taking part in the challenge, just day dreaming really and waiting for the caffeine to kick start my brain, but then one of the boats, instead of passing by, slowed down to a stop.

The guy on the tiller hailed me. "Nice sounding engine, son!"

I turned to look at the puffs of smoke escaping from our exhaust stack then pointed to it. "Are you talking about that?"

"Yes, that. Sounds really healthy."

"Are you serious? Sounds like it's about to die if you ask me."

"Not a chance! That's what a good Bollinder *should* sound like."

"Really? We only managed to get it running about a month ago so we had no idea whether it sounded okay or not."

"Take my word for it. She's a beauty so take good care of her. Those beasts are as rare as rocking horse shit and worth one hell of a lot of money."

"Like how much?"

"In good original condition? I'd say somewhere in the region of between eight and ten grand. What's she running on?"

"Vegetable oil. We get given the spent oil from a café just down the street, we filter it and chuck in in the tank."

"Certainly seems to like it. Cheap too! I best get going. Nice talking to you."

"And you. Good luck with the Challenge!"

*****

I finished my coffee just as Callum appeared so back on with the kettle.

"Who were you talking to? Fuck, I'm tired!"

"Some bloke on a boat commented on our engine."

"Oh yeah? Like, what did he say, scrap it?"

"No, actually he said it sounded really good. He even knew by the sound it makes, what make it is. He told me that Bollinder's should sound like that.

One other thing. He reckons it's worth a pissing fortune!"

"Not ours to sell even if we wanted to, which we don't."

"That's a point? Who does own this building?"

"Ronny. He owns next doors yard as well which is why we don't get any grief."

"Good to know. What's on the first floor?"

"Search me. I don't even know where the stairs are unless they're next door, but anyway, I've never heard anyone up there.

What had you planned for today Ed?"

"I was thinking I really ought to go and see my mother. I mean, she probably doesn't want to see me but I really should make the effort if only once."

"Where is she?"

"She's in the secure psychiatric wing at Good Hope."

"Not far then. We could take a short cut down the towpath past where we were yesterday. That would lead us down to Aston quicker than going by road."

"We? You mean you wanna tag along?"

"Yeah sure, unless you don't want me too?"

"Actually, I could use some moral support, so if you really don't mind?"

"I want to come with you. You shouldn't have to face that all by yourself, and anyhow, you're my boyfriend and that's what boyfriends do isn't it?"

I smiled. "I could get to like being your boyfriend if that's the way you're going to treat me!"

"Yeah well…… I could do so much more for you but……"

"I know Callum but just take it steady. I want but I don't want…… I'm just not sure about, you know, having sex with another boy."

"It wouldn't be sex. I'd like to call it making love, but it doesn't matter 'cos I'm not about to go pushing you into stuff you don't wanna do.

C'mon, let's hit Ronny's and get us some breakfast."

*****

By the time we made it as far as the lock flight, most of the boats had already gone through leaving only the riff-raff and cider junkies wandering around.

"Just ignore them Ed, they're harmless enough. They look and smell like shit but then who are we to go throwing stones. Fuck only knows what tales they could tell if we hung around long enough to listen."

"I know but it's really sad, don't you think?"

"No, I don't think. We all of us have choices, take you as an example. You didn't *have* to leave home? You chose to. Me? Yeah, I had choices, but I always promised myself that no matter what, drugs and booze were never going to play a part in my life, but then you have these blokes. They could go to the Social Services, find a hostel, find a job, but they can't be arsed, instead they beg on the streets and get wrecked on the proceeds."

"But you......"

"Okay already! So I made a bad choice and one that, while you're on the scene will never happen ever again!"

"Whoo, Callum? Don't be so touchy!"

"I mean it, Ed. I'm doing my best to em...... court you here, and I'm never going to win you if I go getting shagged by all in sundry, am I? I'd rather go without than run the risk of fucking this up!"

"Oh shit. No pressure then?"

"Fuck off, Ed! I was trying to be serious!"

"I know, and I appreciate it more than you'll ever know, and by the way, we're together already, so to use one of your favourite expressions, shut the fuck up!"

Callum giggled, and with arms around each-others waists, we walked on.

*****

"Can I see Mrs Anderson please?"

"And, you are?"

"I'm her son, Edward Anderson, and before you ask, this is my em, boyfriend, Callum Lee."

"Wait here please, I think the staff nurse will need to talk to you."

Ten minutes later found us sitting in an office together with a rather attractive nurse.

"Edward? I'm not so sure this is a good idea. Your Mum is mentally highly unstable, given to violent mood swings followed by very emotional outbursts. Sometimes she seems rational, other times she just shuts herself away from reality, so I don't want you to go upsetting yourself."

"Thanks, and I appreciate what you're saying, but Mother hasn't been like my Mum for a couple of years now, so I think I'll be able to cope."

"Well, if you're sure. We have CCTV monitoring her room, so if there're any problems, then we'll be there like a shot but, we don't monitor any conversations. Just bare in mind what I've just told you, you might not like what you find."

*****

"Hello Mum. I thought I'd come to see how you're doing."

My mother was sitting down and gazing out of the window, not that there was much to see except for high-rise apartment blocks and industrial units.

She turned and looked at me for a moment before resuming her original pose.

"Oh, it's you. What do you want?"

"Yes, well, it's nice to see you too. I just told you, I've come to see how you are."

"Well, now you've seen, why don't you leave me alone."

"Because…… because you're my mother, you carried me for nine months, went through the pain of giving me life, I'm your son, for fuck's sake, that's why?"

"There's no need for filthy language, I know who you are, and for what it's worth, whatever debt you mistakenly think you owe me is paid."

"Yeah, okay, but I think we've gone past the point where you can tell me what I'm allowed to say or do, you abdicated that right the moment you hooked up with that Vincent."

She ignored that comment but changed tack.

"Who's that boy you've got with you?"

"This is Callum and he's my boyfriend, like you're really interested!"

"Boyfriend. Like father, like son. What a disappointment you are."

"And I should be proud of *you?* You shit on my life, abused and tormented me, found yourself an animal to live with who

ALSO beat me up, busted up everything I owned, you smashed up our home and pumped yourself so full of drugs and alcohol I could hardly recognise you? Get a fucking life mother?"

There was almost no response. My mum rocked herself back and forth, but then turned to me.

"I think you'd better go now. I don't want to see you again, do you understand?"

"So that's it, is it? Go away and pretend nothing is the matter, pretend I never had a loving family?"

"I have no recollections of those times. Now is now, here is here, and here's where I will die. Go and see the Matron, she has something for you, and while you're there, tell her I NEED MY METHADONE!! NOW, GET *OUT AND DON'T EVER COME BACK!!"*

*****

Callum lead me to a quiet spot behind the bandstand in Aston Park overlooking Aston Villa's football stadium where I cried...... then bawled my eyes out.

Callum said nothing but let me get the negativity out of my system, then once I'd calmed down, he gave me a cuddle then suggested that we made tracks for home and some hot black coffee.

*****

It was late by the time we were all bedded down for the night, obviously the party spirit had lasted through Boxing Day, but tomorrow would be business as usual, whatever 'usual' meant for us, and to be perfectly honest, I really didn't want to know what these kids got up to.

Sometimes one of them would disappear for a couple of days then return with stories of being arrested for some minor crime, taken to court, put into care before promptly escaping. Some would disappear never to be seen again, maybe opting for life within the care system, maybe moving to a different city, who knows, but then I had my own future to think about and perversely, that of Callum's as I wasn't going to abandon him to life as a rent boy. I felt things for him, a closeness and affection I'd never experienced for another person before.

Sleep finally overtook me not waking until eight the following morning with Callum giving me a shake.

"Got you some coffee, sleepy-head. Want anything for breakfast or shall we go to Ronny's a bit later?"

"Ronny's. What's the weather doing?"

"Pissing it down if you really wanna know, plus the wind has backed to the north east so I reckon we'll get snow later."

"Footprint problems then?"

"Nah, I don't think so, but we might talk to Ronny to find out if he's happy for us to make up a proper door rather than that sodding hole in the wall. If the temperature really does decide to fall, it'll be impossible to keep the place even slightly warm what with that draught."

"Double edged sword. It'll stop the draught but an open invitation for people to come snooping around."

"I've got a combination door lock so we can come and go as we please, the regular lads can have the code, but it'll keep the riff-raff out. Sorted!"

"We are the riff-raff or had you forgotten."

"Alright, smart-arse. It'll keep the *other* riff-raff out!"

"That's better.

Changing the subject? When we get down to Ronny's, I ought to look at that letter that Matron gave me. I can't imagine it's like good news but she seemed to think it was important."

Chapter Eleven.

The more I read, the more I understood. Events that, at the time had seemed insignificant, were now slotting into place like pieces of a jigsaw puzzle.

On opening the envelope, I found not one, but three separate smaller ones and instructions as to the order in which they should be read.

The first of these was a letter written by the Chief Clinician of the unit where my Mother was being looked after. I had to read it twice before I fully understood the implications, and once the information had finally hit home, I placed the letter on the table and just stared out of the window in disbelief.

Callum was quick to read my reaction and reaching for my hand said, "I was going to ask if you're okay but I know you're not. Do you want to tell me what it said or shut up maybe?"

"I'll read it to you. Just give me a minute please?"

I wasn't upset, in truth I think I was in shock as this was absolutely the last thing I'd expected to hear.

I took a deep breath, picked up the letter and began to read it out loud.

'Dear Edward.

By virtue of the fact that you're in receipt of this letter means you have visited this wing in order to see your Mother.

As you are no doubt aware, she was admitted into intensive care following a drug overdose and that in itself is a very serious matter but made more so due to the following.

The cocktail of narcotics ingested combined with a large quantity of alcohol, all of which, habitually consumed led to acute kidney failure.

Your Mother was already suffering from alcohol related liver disease, in her case Sclerosis, and these factors combined with her already seriously compromised immune response means that effective treatment is not available to her.

I feel that it is necessary to see you at the earliest opportunity in order that I can personally explain to you where we go from here. Therefore, if you could call my secretary on the number shown below, I would much appreciate it.

One further matter. I would respectfully suggest that you refrain from opening the other envelopes until such time as we meet. I am aware of the contents, and so to facilitate your full understanding of these, I will arrange for our resident solicitor to be on hand.

Yours sincerely,

Dr A.P.J. Burnham.'

"Could you translate that into English Ed?"

"Yeah, well, simply put…… my dear Mother has managed to total her kidneys by taking drugs, booze has fucked her liver, but I've no idea what he's talking about when he mentions her already compromised immune response but it doesn't sound too hopeful.

I'd better make that call."

*****

"Dr Burnham's secretary, how may I help you?"

"Oh, Good Morning. My name is Edward Anderson and I've received a letter from you asking me to make an appointment to see Dr Burnham."

"You must be Ellen Anderson's son, is that correct?"

"Yes, that's me."

"When are you available to come to the clinic? Dr Burnham has consultations all morning but he could see you at around two-thirty this afternoon if that's convenient?"

"I'll be there, but there's just one other matter. He mentioned having a solicitor present."

"It's all on file so I'll see if I can arrange it. If there's a problem, can I get you on this number?"

"Oh, sure. It never gets switched off."

"Thank you. We'll see you this afternoon then. Good bye."

I breathed a massive sigh of relief.

"Good! I hate waiting around. In a few hours' time, I'll know the worst and then it's up to me to deal with it."

"Us to deal with it, Ed. You're not alone, remember?"

"Yeah, sorry. I keep forgetting. I feel as if I should be emotional but nothing's happening. She's dying, I know that, so why do I

feel calm? Most kids of my age would be mortified but I'm......
oh, I don't know."

"Numb?"

"Yeah, good word. Numb does it for me, but I don't even feel
guilty about feeling numb! Crazy!"

"Street life has a nasty habit of hardening you. I've seen things
that would turn an adult's stomach to jelly, but I just take it as the
normal process of life, walk away and forget about it.

Sometimes I wish I could cry, but it's something that's alien to
me. I feel the urge, but then there's nothing there, like I'm conditioned not to feel sorrow or remorse.

Do you remember me telling you how Buba cried when you
were reading to us? I envied him! I wanted to feel how he felt, I
wanted to feel so sad but *I couldn't!* So a girl got eaten by a shark,
so what! People get run over by a truck, so what! I've...... lost
my soul somewhere along the way, Ed."

"We better go and find it then! I don't want a boyfriend who
lacks compassion!"

*****

"Thank you for coming to see me, Edward. I can only begin to
understand how you must be feeling, so if you have questions,
anything at all, then please feel free to ask me. I don't like this aspect of my job but I'll cut to the chase.

Edward? Your Mum is dying. There's no easy way of breaking
this news to you, so I beg forgiveness if my manner is direct and
to the point, but perhaps you'll find it easier to accept it this way
rather than me running around the houses."

"It's okay Doctor. I think I'd worked that out for myself. I do have questions though?"

"Ask away."

"Drugs and alcohol...... the effects I can understand, but then you went on to say in your letter something about my Mother's immune response being already weakened.

What did you mean by this?"

"You obviously didn't read the letter in the second envelope. That's good, because I can give you the clinical answer before you read the historical.

Your Mum is HIV positive. She's been taking anti-retroviral medication which, under most normal circumstances, would extend her life almost indefinitely. Unfortunately, the fact that she is...... how can I put this...... an alcoholic drug addict, rendered this medication completely useless. Her HIV status migrated to AIDS for which, so far, there is no remedy.

Do you understand what I'm telling you?"

"Yes...... yes I understand, but you don't just become HIV positive like contracting Flu, so who was responsible? Was it that Vincent?"

"This is where things become very difficult, Edward. You see, your Father had found out that he was HIV positive a few years ago. Obviously he isn't one of my patients so I can't be one hundred percent sure how he's faring, but my understanding is that he's responding well to the medication and should live to a ripe old age. Your Mother knew about her condition before your parents separated, so the likelihood is, your Father was the cause of her contracting the infection.

The man you mentioned, Vincent Connor? He discharged himself just as soon as he was able. He was never tested by this hospital, but if he and your Mother were sharing needles, then it's very possible that he too is infected."

"Oh, my God. That explains so much. The fights, the constant arguments and why my Dad left us."

"I think that's all part of the letter that your Mother wrote to you. That, together with the third envelope came at a time when she was mentally stable and we were able to put things in place that would guarantee your future, but that's something Mr Allen, our solicitor will run through with you a bit later. For now it might be a good idea to read your Mothers letter."

Again, for Callum's benefit, I read it out loud.

> 'Dear Edward.
> Now I'm sane enough to write to you, I have no idea where to begin, so perhaps I should start by telling you something that for the last few years I've not been able to do.
> This brief respite from hallucinations, self-pity and paranoia have made me come to the realisation that I've failed you in the most awful way imaginable. You're my son, and despite my behaviour of the past few years, I do, and always have loved you. Please Edward, you have to believe me. Sitting here now, I have an

understanding of how cruel I have been, but my addiction to drugs and alcohol robbed me of my conscience, I was living from fix to fix, nothing else mattered, only the overwhelming need to escape from reality, to forget I was suffering from that horrible disease, but then I'd come down and that need was doubly important, like an endless spiral into hopelessness.

I can only imagine that it was you who called the authorities, and I'm pleased you did. You gave me an opportunity to look at myself if only for a short while, to see what I've thrown away and to give me the chance to tell you those things that most children take for granted, the unconditional love of a Mother towards her offspring.

I have been in contact with your Father so he's aware of the situation, but he's leaving it up to you to get in touch with him if you so wish, otherwise he will continue to pay all the utility bills, your allowance together with my divorce settlement will be paid into my bank account to which you are now the sole signatory.

In the other envelope you will find all the legal documentation, an application form for a charge card on my account together with various other bits and pieces, so I strongly recommend that you have a qualified solicitor explain everything to you.

Edward, my condition will rapidly deteriorate. I will become angry, completely lacking all other emotions, so I *must* take this opportunity to re-iterate just how much I love you and just how much I'd give to be able to turn back the clock and be the Mum you always should've had, but I can't undo what is already done.

Please find it in your heart to forgive me?

Find happiness in no matter what you do or how your life works out. Find love and always cherish that person no matter what.

Mum.

*****

"Any chance of a glass of water please?"

"I'll have one brought through for you. How are you holding up?"

"Okay actually. I think that deep down I always knew she loved me, but with home life being how it was, well, it wasn't possible to see beyond the situation as it was at that time.

She said that her condition would rapidly deteriorate, so does that mean she'll never be lucid again?"

"She will have brief periods of normality, but they'll become less and briefer as time progresses. Why do you ask?"

"Because I want to write her a letter, but there would be little point if she wasn't able to understand it."

"Do it, and I'll make sure that she reads it when the opportunity presents itself."

"I'll decide on a form of words and write it tonight once I get back. I've also got a photo I'd like her to have as it reminds me of the happy times when we were a cohesive family. I'll mention it in my note and say that this is the sort of thing I'll always cling onto rather than the upsetting things."

"However you wish to play it. Are you feeling able to talk to our solicitor or would you rather leave it for now?"

"I might just as well get it out of the way now, if that's okay. I hate the not knowing."

*****

"I'm sorry that you have to deal with these matters, Edward? It's difficult enough for an adult who has been aware of their family members' situation for some time, let alone someone such as yourself, but actually, from the legal standpoint, what has been put in place is relatively simple.

Any questions so far?"

"None that I can think of."

"Right then. I know Dr Burnham has informed you in regard to your Mothers' condition together with the prospect that she hasn't very long to live. She too realises this, and during a sustained period of stability, she elected to write her will setting out her wishes as to how her estate is handled following her demise.

n this regard, her wishes and instructions are simple, you are to be the sole beneficiary of her estate, and until you reach the age of maturity, i.e., eighteen years of age, all such assets will be managed for you by a trust who has a legal obligation to maximise its potential in order that you receive the best return possible come the time.

Any questions?"

"Yes. Who is managing this and what are the costs involved."

"I, or rather my practice is heading it, with a steading hand on the tiller, that of the legal people from the Terrence Higgins Trust together with your Mothers' bank Manager. You are in very capable hands."

"But how much is this costing?"

"The Terrence Higgins Trust is covering all the costs, Edward."

"The Terrence Higgins Trust? Who are they?"

"They're an organisation dedicated to assist those suffering from AIDS, their families and dependants. If you have trouble coming to terms with your Mothers' illness or your Fathers' condition, they are in a position to help and guide you.

How old are you Edward?"

"I turned sixteen on December 13th."

"Right. In that case, you are old enough to live on your own should you so wish. Many youngsters of your age do so quite happily, so if you felt like you wanted to move back in to the family home, then there's no reason why you shouldn't."

"Except for one. The entire place was trashed during one of their drink and drug sessions, and to be perfectly honest, I dread to think what I might find if I go rooting around.

There are bits and pieces that could be sold, but the rest I'd want shot of. Furniture, beds, carpets and curtains, everything out and possibly be treated as contaminated waste just in case there are used needles kicking about."

"Your local authority will have specialist teams to do that for you. Was there any structural damage?"

"Only my bedroom window. That got smashed in, although God only knows how as it was triple glazed, but none-the-less, it is no more."

"Okay. Fixable and something that should be actioned quickly. Any questions?"

"Two. It sounds like I'm money-grabbing, but could my Mothers' will be challenged in court?"

"By whom? Do you have any close relatives on your Mothers' side?"

"No, none. She was an only child. I was thinking more about my Father."

"Technically he's no longer family as your parents divorced. As your natural Father, he could try for custody, and if it were successful, then he would have a call on your Mothers' estate, but only enough to support you until you reach the age of eighteen, but, and it's a big but, no court in the land would find in his favour. He walked away from you and your Mother for reasons we can only speculate about. He has never tried to contact you, has he? Birthday card, Christmas card?"

"Nothing."

"So, an absent family member smells the chance of clawing back something from a failed relationship thus depriving the legally appointed beneficiary of his entitlement?

Not a cats' chance in hell, Edward. I've already told you that you are perfectly entitled to live on your own now you're sixteen, and there's absolutely nothing he can do, legally or otherwise, that can alter that, so custody is, simply put, a non-starter, and without that, he has no claim on your Mothers' estate."

"Thank you. My life is complicated enough without worrying about his interference."

"You said you had two questions?"

"You answered both. The second was about a possible custody case."

"Good stuff. I'll make enquiries about getting your house cleared and the repairs carried out. Is this your mobile number?"

"Yeah. You can reach me on that anytime, but I need to be there when it's cleared so I can select what's kept and what's chucked out."

"I'll make very sure you're kept up to speed. We'll need your keys for access anyway."

Chapter Twelve.

The walk home was subdued. I was in my own little world and Callum had the common sense not to question me. He knew me well enough by now that given time, I'd open up to him, but for now I had issues to deal with, not the least of these being the AIDS thing and whether or not I should try and make contact with my Father.

Another thing that I'd learned was, that being sixteen, I wasn't breaking any laws by not living at home without adult supervision. I guessed that I was also entitled to leave school, so getting around during the day wouldn't pose a problem. I'd have to register for work or get into full time college education, an idea I much preferred as it would still mean I had time to help some of the younger kids with their reading, writing and maths.

I needed to talk with someone, someone who wasn't involved or wouldn't take sides, a totally independent individual who would listen to me rather than lecture me.

I decided to sound Ronny out, he and I had always had something of a rapport. We had talked about so many things in the past, nothing directly connected to my situation, but things in general, and I felt as if I could trust him and more importantly, give me the benefit of his knowledge without being biased one way or the other.

Whatever. I had to tell Callum how I felt about stuff. He was standing there foursquare behind me. He was like a loyal puppy who never so much as questioned my actions, supported me at times when I can only imagine he felt like a fish out of water, but still, he was always there for me and I never wanted it to be any different. Damn it, I really did love him, but my middle class and prudish upbringing told me that expressing that love physically was wrong, even if I found myself thinking about that aspect of our relationship more and more.

I had ponded this situation many times, but the only conclusion I had reached was that girls didn't do it for me.

I liked them well enough...... well, what dealings I'd had with them were nice enough, I liked them but...... but I didn't fancy them, and at sixteen years of age, surely that's weird?

Callum had struck a chord in my heart. He was a complex individual though. One moment he'd be bouncing around playing silly games with our younger lads, the next he could be serious and thoughtful, but always his kindness and tolerance towards even the biggest idiot shone through.

He was an organiser, where he set the pace, others followed his lead. Even the most menial of jobs around our squat were actioned by him, setting an example to even the laziest of our number. His infectious fun-attitude rubbed off on everyone, but then I'd find him looking at me, a gentle smile holding my eyes for a fraction of a second and I'd melt inside.

*****

The weather turned really nasty. The cold penetrated everything, the fire making things slightly more tolerable, but we were rattling through coal at an alarming rate to the point where as fast as the kids nicked it from next door, we burnt it.

"Shit, Callum? If we carry on like this, the waterways people will suss it out and call the police!"

"No they won't. I think they'll be glad to see the back of it."

"What makes you think that?"

"It's been here for years. They bought it to sell on to boaters but then the law changed. Boaters can only use certified smoke-free coal and this stuff isn't certified meaning they'd be breaking the law if they hived it off. Anyway, I caught the tail end of a conversation the other day. Some big-wig from the waterways was telling Ronny that they were out of there at the end of January but he had a problem with this coal, and like he didn't know what to do with the stuff. Ronny told him it was okay to leave it where it was, then he winked at me, you know, one of 'those' winks.

It's ours for the taking Ed!"

"No shit!"

"Absolutely! No shit! Mr Waterways is one happy bunny and we stay warm...... well, warmish."

"In that case, we better get the lads on the job a bit later. Maybe we could open up the other fireplace and really get the place stoked up."

"What other fireplace? There's only the one in here?"

"Wrong. I saw it when we tested the electrics. This used to be two rooms and each had its own fireplace, but then when it was knocked through, I guess one was blocked off, you can see the difference in the brick bonding plus I looked at the roof...... two chimneys!"

"Well, fuck me!"

"I normally charge shit-loads for that, but beings as it's you, Callum? No charge!"

"Sod off Ed. Don't play with my emotions, okay?"

"I wasn't playing…… I…… I think I need to get closer, we need to get closer…… that is if you still want to?"

"If this is because you're upset about your Mum, then no, I don't think we should, but……"

"This hasn't anything to do with that! No, that's not true either. It *does* have something to do with it, but only because she said something, something that for once made sense."

"But you didn't see her, so what are you driving at?"

"In her letter to me. In that letter she told me to find love, and when I found it, I was to cherish it, honour it and stick with that person. What's more, she also said 'who ever that might be'. It was as if she was giving me her blessing to find happiness in whatever way it manifested itself. I don't get all excited by girls, but I see you looking at me sometimes and my stomach turns over. I can't explain what or how I feel, it's sort of alien to me, but I do know that you turn me on and I want you to do stuff with me and me to you."

Callum turned away and shook his head. "I want you too, you know that for, fuck's sake, but…… look, Ed? I've done the rounds. I know all about sex with another guy, but you? Have you really thought about what you've just said?

I don't want you on the rebound, I love you too much for that. If we get together then I want to be absolutely sure it's what you want, not only for your sake, but…… but I have feelings too, and I don't want to get hurt."

"This isn't a new thing. I've known for ages that my feelings towards you were the way they are, but I've always been brought up to believe that homosexuality was a sin but I see things differently now. We hang labels, unfair labels on relationships that don't conform to the majority view. Society used to mock people who said the world was round, they were seen as heretics, anti-God trouble makers, but we now know they were right, so why not this? I didn't wake up one day and think to myself, 'I know? Today I'm going to covert to gay!' That's so much bullshit. I've fallen in love with another guy in much the same way I could've fallen in love with a girl. Isn't that my normality?"

"I want it to be, but just for now, let's not go bull at a gate at this, Ed? Slowly, gently gets my vote, okay?"

"Deal. I'll be in your hands."

"Not now, not tonight, maybe not this week, but we'll both know when the time is right. I want you to want me, so nothing gets rushed."

*****

"Look, I'm really sorry to burden you like this, Ronny, but I need advice and I couldn't think of anyone else I trusted."

"Me? You flatter me, Ed. Look, my night girl is due in at any time, so let me get these meals out and on the table, so when she gets here we can talk somewhere less public."

Eventually Ronny appeared and with me slightly relieved, we went through to his office where he sat me down.

"Alright. So, what's eating at you?"

"Stuff. Stuff I don't know how to deal with. I thought I was getting to grips with life, but then, just as I was starting to feel hopeful, something comes along and kicks me in the guts."

"I think they call that the reality of life my friend, but I know you well enough to realise this isn't something insignificant.

Tell me all about it."

I went through the entire thing from my Father doing a runner right through to the news from the clinic.

Ronny studied his hands before looking at me.

"That's one fucked up story, Ed, and to be truthful, I'm not so sure I'm the right person you should be talking to. I don't have any experience when it comes to this kind of thing. My life has been all about staying afloat and keeping the family together, but shit? I wouldn't know where to start or how to advise you when this sort of thing happens. Can it wait for twenty-four hours to give me time to think about it?"

"Twenty-four, forty-eight, who cares. I just need answers."

"I know you do, but just as a starter, you know that all of you are welcome to stay right where you are. I admit I had misgivings once the numbers started to increase but so far as I'm aware, there has been no bother, no acrimony, so I've no intention of kicking anyone out. Go back once you've finished your meal and I'll try to come up with some answers in the next couple of days.

Just one other matter while you're here, Ed? Callum said something about fitting a door where that hole in the wall is. Without wanting to sound mean, I'd prefer that the damn thing was bricked up rather than making it even more obvious that the place is being used, but I do understand that you want to keep out the draught, so if you can wait a couple of weeks, the waterways people will be gone and I'll arrange for you to have keys to their old place so you can knock through where the old internal door used to be, use both places if you want, no one else is going to."

"That's very generous of you. Thanks."

"That's okay. Buildings are best when they're in use. I can only imagine that the fires you've been burning constantly have dried the place out no end. Then there's that old engine and generator? I nearly sold it for scrap a few years ago!"

"You did? Christ, Ronny? Have you any idea just how much it's worth?"

"Not a clue, but I imagine you're about to tell me."

"Between five and ten grand in decent working order."

"Nice to know, but don't worry because so long as you kids need it, it's going nowhere, but the one next door.....?"

"There's another one?"

"Oh, yes, but I had it bricked up when the waterways decided to rent the place. The same with the first floor. They didn't want to pay the rent on a two story property so I wasn't about to give them access. I'll have it all opened up as it should be once they've disappeared."

"What's up there?"

"I haven't got the first idea, I've never been up there. I bought the entire block as an investment believing the City Council would regenerate the area, but put until now they've past this part of the canal frontage by bless 'em!"

"I bet you're not pleased about that then?"

"I don't mind. I was left some money, and it was a case of sticking it in the bank where I'd get sod-all interest worth talking about or buy property where given time, I should see some sort of return. Buildings, like everything else, are better off being used rather than letting them rot, so if it gives you lot more space, you might just as well use it."

*****

I walked back feeling a lot more positive. I had straightened things out with Callum and now I had Ronny on side, so, buoyed up with enthusiasm, I enlisted some volunteers and made a start on opening up the second fireplace while some of the other lads nipped next door for more coal, now safe in the knowledge that we could take it without any nasty consequences.

Removing the brickwork was child's play, it was what we discovered lurking behind them that took us by surprise. An old cooking range that had to be over one hundred years old and seemingly in good enough condition.

Callum was especially vocal.

"Shit! Do you realise what this means? We won't have to go out in the cold and rain to cook our grub! We can do it in-house so to speak. Fucking rock on!"

"What sort of state is the firebox in? The fire bricks might've collapsed for all we know?"

He took a look and pronounced them as being soft but intact.

"Light a small fire. That might just dry them out sufficiently enough, but if not, then there's some fire clay left over from when I had to patch up our original fireplace plus there's probably more next door, 'cos that's where I nicked it from! The flue looks in good enough condition which is good 'cos I haven't a clue how we could fix it otherwise.

Want me to set a fire Ed?"

"Nothing ventured I guess."

"And loads to be gained. This beauty is made of cast iron, and once it gets warm, it'll kick heat into the place much more efficiently than the old fireplace ever did!"

A crowd of us cleared up the debris while Callum sorted out laying a small fire, and once he'd set a match to it, we went out canal-side and looked up at the chimney.

It had smoke wafting up into the sky then slowly dissipating to a sight heat haze as the wood burned away leaving our uncertified smokeless coal to do its work.

After about two hours, the difference in temperature was noticeable, but Callum was cautious about pushing our luck by building up a larger blaze.

"Leave it for tonight, then tomorrow once it's burned itself out, we can take a second look at the firebricks and patch them up if we need to."

Buba stood there, his assumed role as the community cook taking his thinking to another level.

"Shit, man? This gives me so many ideas! Ronny has so much left-over grub, he either feeds all of us or chucks it away. If we get a huge pot, we can take it off his hands, chuck it in with some seasoning, and hey-presto, an ever-lasting and nutritious stockpot,

constantly on the go, hot food for the taking with the added bonus, we get Ronny's over-cater to add to it each day."

"What, like chuck everything in? Potatoes, vegetables......
everything?"

,"Yeah! That's the beauty of a stockpot man? Mince it all up,
keep it ticking over on a low heat and you've a meal in a bowl.
Good for you and very filling. Bring it on!"

"You'll have to figure out how to bake bread next!"

"I already know, smart arse. Gimme the ingredients and the
rest is down to my fingers."

*****

The next morning with the firebricks declared fit for use, we
put a match to a bigger fire, and once it had caught, I turned to
Callum and told him I had to go back home for a few days.

"I need to organise things like that bank account, get the Council to empty the house of all the soft furnishings, carpets and the
like, then have someone look at my bedroom window. Just for
now I'm going to board it up to stop the place getting any damper
than it already is then decide where to go from there.

Will you come with me?"

"Yeah sure. It would be good to get away from this place for a
while, but if you're going to strip the place of furniture, where do
propose that we sleep?"

"My Mother bought me a new mattress for my bed. It never
got further than the garage, so once everything is out of the way
then we bring it in and use the main bedroom. I don't think it's
necessary to get shot of the hardware, just anything that might be
contaminated, so like carpets and mattresses, easy chairs and so

on. Bed linen I'll take a close look at, but the clean stuff should be fine, and we have spare pillows in the attic which I vacuum packed.

What I could really do with is a laptop, then I could sell all the clothing on Ebay, then once everything is done...... I guess it's a case of deciding what I do next."

"You reckon you'll stay there?"

"No chance! God knows, if I could, I'd sell the fucking place, but I can't until I'm eighteen, so I really don't know what to do for the best."

"Rent it out?"

"Not mine to rent out. The power of attorney rests with...... *Callum? You're a genius!* The solicitor at the clinic together with the doctor and Mother's bank manager have a duty to maximise her assets. They won't want the place to stand empty, will they?"

"Like the posters point out. 'Watch out, there are thieves about'."

"Meaning?"

"They just might take the money and run."

"I was told that Mother's estate was being held in trust until I was eighteen when I would become the sole beneficiary. I am also allowed an input as to how it's invested although I can't override their decisions, but if they *did* do a runner, I'd have a pretty good case against them."

"Trust no one and you won't ever be disappointed, Ed."

"There are times when you have few options open to you. They're trusted by the hospital, so not being aware of any good reasons not to, I have to trust them, but don't make me paranoid! I'll go and tell some of the guys we'll be away for a couple of days, so go get a coat so we can get out of here pronto."

I found Pip and Tiny in the courtyard and explained where we were going. Pip offered his services if we needed him, so I promised to call him should the need arise, and with that done, we left for the station and the trip back to Solihull.

Chapter Thirteen.

S ix months of growing my hair out paid off as there were faces on the train that I recognised. I ignored them and nothing was said although there might've been flashes of curiosity.

I let us in through the front door, picked up the post and went through to the kitchen. The house was just as we'd left it so I made us some coffee and settled down to open the collection of junk mail of which there were stacks of the stuff. Callum walked the house, and declaring it untouched since our last visit, sat down beside me.

"Doesn't it feel weird being back here Ed?"

"Nah, not really. I have good memories as well as bad, so it's not too difficult.

Can I leave you to sort through this crap? Anything in brown or white envelopes or anything with a hand written address, keep, otherwise rip the rest up and bin it. I need to check the garage."

As was the house, the garage was untouched including my mother's little Vauxhall Astra. There was also garden equipment such as a petrol lawn mower and a brand-spanking new cultivator which I remembered my father buying so he could landscape the garden, but…… things turned sour before he had a chance to do anything. Hedge cutters, shears and other bits and pieces hung on the wall, but it meant nothing to me except that the sensation of walking back in time was odd.

I locked up and went back into the house.

Callum was still ploughing his way through the post but looked up at me as I wandered in.

"Everything check out?"

"Yeah. Nothing's changed. Do any of the guys have a drivers licence?"

"I think Pip does what with his Dad being a cabby but you'd have to check with him. Why do you ask?"

"My mother's car. It's still in the garage, and if memory serves, it still has a current test certificate. It's like fuck-all use to me, so if anyone can use it then fine."

"Why don't you sell it and raise some cash?"

"I don't think many people are going to get too excited over a twelve year old Astra with a tiny engine. No, if Pip could use it then great. It'd be something less to worry about."

"You've got a kind heart, did you know that?"

I laughed. "Not me! I'm just being practical. It'll be a year before I'm old enough to drive and by then that car will be past its sell-by date, so why not give it away whilst it still has a useful life."

"I guess. Are you going to call Pip and tell him?"

"In the morning. My first priority is food so I'm going to see what's in the freezer and put something together."

*****

We had become so used to bedding down early, we were ready for sleep by around nine-thirty.

Things got a bit touchy-feely, but instead of rejecting Callum, I found his tender touches erotic, but he held back from actually doing 'stuff'. This made me want him more, but he was being patient, not trying to pressure me, and yes, it made me realise that I wasn't averse to going that bit further with him. He did things to my insides when he looked at me, I sometimes had to turn away in order that he wouldn't see me blush, and very often, if we were holding hands, which we did a lot, I'd get an erection.

There were moments when I'd try to imagine what my life might be like if he disappeared from it. I'd get by, yeah, I would *now,* but I reckoned I'd most likely turn myself in to the authorities without his friendship.

Callum was my support, my backbone and my reason to live.

I loved him.

No doubt about it.

*****

The next morning was all about organising things like getting a house clearance company to get shot of most of the furniture, another phone call to Pip regarding the car to which he said he'd make it to the house that afternoon, then another call to the hospital to check on my mother.

No real change there, just a steady decline not helped by her withdrawal from her drug habit, so most of the time she remained under sedation. I felt as if I should be upset about this, but as it was, she was probably well out of it, in the right place and being cared for by the right people.

Callum wanted to know if I'd had any thoughts about trying to contact my father. Actually, I hadn't given it much thought. I ought to, but then I didn't want him to go interfering in my life. No doubt he'd be very critical about my circumstances and try to convince me to go and live with him, go back to fulltime education and whatever else, but things had moved on, and his attitude I really didn't need.

Pip arrived, and following mugs of tea, he set about giving the car the once-over. I had found all the documentation such as a valid test certificate and road tax, both of which were current for the next nine months. The insurance stated that with the owner's consent, anyone who held a UK drivers licence and hadn't been convicted of a motoring offence in the last five years was entitled to drive, so that was something else we didn't have to worry about.

The car didn't take much to get it started, bloody good little machines these Vauxhall's, so after a trip around town and a fuel fill, Pip declared himself as my official driver.

The window people arrived and repaired my bedroom window, so I ramped up the heating to finally dry the place out. Pip stayed overnight as the house clearance people were due the next day and his help would be gratefully accepted, with the added bonus of a ride back to the squat once they'd left.

He also told us that Buba had been taken on by Ronny as a short order cook which would give him a small but steady income, British Waterways had all but left next door so in a few days we would be able to move in.

The clearance went well and I actually got paid for some of the better items, but after they'd left, the place looked soulless and barren.

Time to go and think about what to do with the place, but first do some of the odd jobs like repairing the fence that backed on to the playing field, trim back the grass that was about to overtake the place and generally make the outside look like somebody cared about it.

All the time we'd been doing this, I never once caught sight of our neighbours and I wondered if they'd caught on to what had gone on during Mum and Vincent's time spent there. Their rows had been violent, the noise, despite the house being set in its own grounds, must have been heard, but still, with all the activity, Callum, Pip plus me and a few others being around, they never so much as enquired.

I locked up and Pip drove us back to Digbeth and our squat.

"Where are you planning on keeping it Pip? Can't hardly keep it on the road can you?"

"No, that's just asking for trouble, so I'd thought about asking Ronny if I could keep it in his yard, then once we've got access to the old B.W. yard next to us, keep it there."

"Tax, insurance? They've also go to be taken into consideration?

"Easy done Ed.   There's that Chinese restaurant, the Indian and the Bangladeshi place. I reckon if I handled it right, I might get work doing take-away deliveries, and if any of the kids need a lift, charge them a couple of quid and job's a good-un."

"Thought it all through then?"

"Yeah, well, you have to living on the streets. See an opportunity to make some cash and grab it. That's how we manage to survive, Ed."

"I've a lot to learn. I must think of ways to earn something, 'cos I'm not being very productive as things stand."

"Piss off! Most of the kids can make it past reading the headlines, count the money in their pockets and write a letter? That's all because of you and the time you spent with all of us, me included, so what's that if not productive?

The generator, the new fireplace, this car and...... and...... just the fact that most of us are still here like a real community must tell you summat? For maybe the first time that most of them can remember, they're happy, settled, warm and amongst friends. This has to be your biggest contribution ever!

When was the last time you heard about any of them getting arrested? Not for months right? You've made them look beyond petty theft, prostituting themselves or whatever, so now they see that there *can be a different way!*"

"Not all my doing Pip."

"Okay, maybe not, but you planted an idea in their heads, gave them hope, showed them love and spent shit-loads of time with them teaching them how to read and write, do sums and so on, and the end result is, they began helping themselves instead of doing fuck-all. Christ, Ed?"

"Okay already, but I'd still like to contribute something, you know, financially?"

"It's not just cash though, nice as it is. The car for starters. You gave it to me, but I would rather look upon it as a shared resource, something that could be used for the benefit of all of us. Then there's the old generator. It was your idea to try and coax it back to life so now we have electricity, cheap electricity to boot.

You found the second fireplace so now we can cook indoors rather than freezing our bits off and doing it outside, and then there's one other thing. Ronny came to see what Buba was doing with all the leftovers. He tried the stockpot and loved it and that's how come he offered him a job.

All these things are more valuable than money, Ed. We're now operating as a unit, a cohesive group of kids working together rather than ships passing in the night, there are things happening, things you don't know about."

"Such as?"

"Two of the boys were doing a recce of the scrapyard and found an automatic washing machine, so under the cover of darkness, they nicked it thinking that the stainless steel drum and the copper windings off the motor could raise some cash, but when they stripped it down, the only problem with it was a snapped drive belt, so finding a similar machine, they took the belt, refitted it to theirs, so now, once BW have buggered off finally, we have laundry facilities and the luxury of clean clothes!"

"They'll be stealing a tumble drier next!"

"Yeah they most likely would if they could find one but it doesn't really matter. We've seen the worst of the winter, the weather will be improving from here on in so things can dry outside."

*****

The days that followed saw a flurry of activity next door as the Waterways people did a final tidy-up before they left.

Most of the gear they loaded onto a barge – we kept a low profile but watched from a distance, interested, not in what they were taking but what they weren't taking, such as two very large plastic water barrels, a couple of wheelbarrows, pickaxes and shovels, bags of cement, builders bags full of sand and pea gravel and a huge selection of builders planks.

One man was checking off a list as the loading progressed, so I assumed that anything that didn't appear on the inventory got left behind no matter if it was serviceable or not, but then one morning the barge had gone. They had left, finally giving us the run of the place.

Buba came back one lunchtime and complete with keys, we made our first exploratory visit inside the building. The interior had been well maintained. The walls were painted with whitewash as were the ceilings, the floor had been coated with floor paint but otherwise they'd left nothing except a large cardboard box in which we found lightbulbs, hundreds of the things and all brand new.

"Why didn't they take these, Ed?"

"Fucked if I know, Pip, but my Dad used to moan on about how accountants like an uncomplicated life. They have a list of what they know was here, and anything that didn't appear on it would mess up their books if it was taken. Maybe as these lightbulbs weren't shown as on stock, it was less of a hassle just to leave them behind."

"Good for us though. Lightbulbs are expensive."

*****

A tour of the other rooms told much the same story – the place had been stripped clean.

We managed to identify what keys fitted which locks. The front door, the yard gates, the door that gave access to the dock and an outbuilding which yielded a few more surprises.

Aside from loads of space to garage the Astra, there were unopened cans of engine oil, hand tools such as a socket set, spanners, screwdrivers, a large workbench complete with vice, two fifty metre extension cables and a petrol cement mixer, which although looked as if it had seen better times, might well be serviceable.

A door at the rear of the building had been padlocked shut, but failing to find a key that fitted it, what was behind that door would remain a mystery for the time being.

Back in the main building, some of the lads had found the door which we thought would lead to the stairs to the first floor. This had also been padlocked, and again, not being able to find the key meant a visit to Ronny later.

We found another door which when we opened it, all we found was a brick wall. We assumed (correctly), this gave access to our squat, so armed with lump hammers and builder's chisels found in amongst the selection of tools in the outbuilding, we made a start on opening it up.

We worked on this for most of the day with some of the boys barrowing the old bricks and stacking them into neat piles on the dock for reuse when Ronny bricked up the hole in the wall.

We uncovered two further fireplaces, one very similar to our original one next door, and another which had a furnace set into it, although its purpose wasn't immediately obvious.

Mid evening saw Buba return from his stint at Ronny's café. He told us that the keys needed to gain access to the first floor and the space at the end of the outbuilding couldn't be found, however Ronny would get his hands on a bolt cutter for us to use.

This he delivered the following day so we tackled the padlocks that secured the door to the first floor rather than further exploring the outbuilding.

We had wondered what we'd find up there, probably nothing of interest, most likely empty but it wasn't. Far from it.

"What the fuck is this kit Ed?"

"I haven't got a clue. It's an engineering workshop of sorts, but I've no idea what half of this stuff is used for." I pointed to a couple of machines. "Those are lathes for turning metal, that's a power saw and that thing there is a milling machine. I know 'cos we had something like them at school but they were modern whereas these are seriously old. As for that beast...... oh, and that thing over there? Don't ask, 'cos I really don't know."

We began to search through cupboards and drawers uncovering all manner of things such as cutting bits for the lathes, what we assumed were cutters for the milling machine together with saw blades and hand tools, but then Tiny made another discovery.

"Hey. Take a gander at this. It looks like a catalogue or something, but it's faded and I can't make it out."

It was falling apart, damp and rotten, so we carefully placed it on one of the work benches before studying it.

"Don't try turning the pages or it'll get fucked for sure. There are ways of preserving this sort of thing, so for now, just try to make out what it says on the front cover."

Bit by bit we managed to make out what was printed.

Myton Bolts and Rivets Limited.
28 – 32 Bishops Wharf Lane
Digbeth
Birmingham
Suppliers of fastenings to boat-building yards
and similar industries.

"Well if nothing else, that gives us something to research."

"How do we do that Ed?"

"Visit libraries and museums. There will be records of this company somewhere, what they did, when they started and when and why they shut up shop, but first we ought to tell Ronny. He does own this stuff after all."

*****

"Sorry, boys, but for the life of me I can't get excited about it. It looks to me as if it was mothballed decades ago, and aside from the interest factor, this junk won't be worth anything other than its scrap value, so if you want to have a dig around, then you carry on.

It does answer one question though. I had wondered what the purpose of the second engine was. It doesn't have an alternator strapped to it like the one next door, it had been used as a belt driven power chain, presumably to drive the shafts that power this stuff.

Like I said. – Interesting, but Birmingham was the engineering hub of the country from the early nineteenth Century until the mid-twentieth Century, and so there are probably dozens of old and forgotten workshops dotted around the city."

"But we do have your permission to find out more?"

"You go ahead, but if you're thinking about getting this lot up and running then please be careful. Everything looks as if it's driven from that main shaft up there, and then there are slipped belts with tensioners to each individual machine. Those belts are probably shot to bits, and if they spit? Well, you might get very badly injured."

Chapter Fourteen.

We transferred to the new building pretty much immediately, then once the hole in the wall had been bricked up, some of the boys made a start of preparing the walls and ceiling to take a coat of whitewash. Callum was in charge of looking at the fireplaces in the new building. The first one needed an amount of work before it was usable, but the furnace one was alright, but in this instance, we found something else as it had been modified to incorporate a back-boiler and convection-fed hot water tank. This fed wash basins and a crude but effective shower.

Ronny told us that British Waterways were going to pay the electricity bill until the end of the quarter and then he would get it disconnected, install an isolator so we could feed power from our generator into the new building. This left me time to further investigate Myton.

*****

"Here you go. I've found something."

Pip, Tiny and I had been trawling through records held in Birmingham Municipal Museum.

"Myton Bolts and Rivets Limited. Company first registered on the 14th August 1879. Trading address; 28 – 32 Bishops Wharf, Birmingham.

It goes on to say that said company was owned by Messrs Michael and Thomas Myton who manufactured and traded in securing's and fixings for industry with note to boat building and repair. They gained a reputation for high quality goods, and business flourished when in 1899 they incorporated a wet dock to berth their own cargo vessel to enable ease of transport of their products.

In 1914 and the outbreak of WWI, production was given over to the manufacture of light armaments and worked closely with the Birmingham Small Arms Company (BSA).

This association lasted until the cessation of hostilities in 1918 when Myton resumed their normal production, but then found the need to diversify, entering in to an arrangement with the Ruston Steam Locomotive Company, for whom they manufactured and supplied specialised and high precision components.

Myton ran a string of boats and transported their products to Ruston's factories in both Doncaster and Wolverton in Buckinghamshire, both of these towns being well served by the canals of the time and business boomed, but then WWII reared its ugly head.

Myton again entered in to a partnership with BSA, but continued supplying Ruston until the end of the war, at which point, BSA entered in to an agreement and that branch, (which incidentally was run from Aston in Birmingham, not Digbeth), was transferred to their ownership for £10.000.)

Myton prospered until the death of Michael, at which point the business shut almost overnight and their business premises sold.

Thomas Myton took retirement, moved to Worcestershire dying aged 91 of natural causes.

Neither of the Myton brothers married.

Michael left his considerable fortune to his brother who, upon his own demise, bequeathed it to good causes, notably the plight of homeless and vulnerable children."

Oh, shit. The silence around the table was deafening, all of us completely lost for words, so I excused myself and asked if the transcript could be copied.

This done, we walked back to the squat in silence, humbled I think does it for me.

*****

That night as we cuddled up together, Callum posed the inevitable question.

"What happens now? So, these wonderful guys had a conscience and we're looking at how they made their money, but……"

"I reckon it's obvious. We have to get their kit back up and running."

"Why? None of us knows how to drive it and anyway, it's so fucking old, it would never cut it in modern industry, so where's the point, Ed?"

"Because we're obligated, that's why! You found next door, maybe by chance, but then I came along. There are now what, twenty of us here? We are living in the building and right underneath the gear that made those two brothers a pile of dosh and when they died, they left it to charity, and more, they left it to us as homeless kids. Sorry, but whether or not you think I'm strange, this has to mean something, Callum."

"I still can't see it. I've had to fight for everything, I've taken unbelievable risks...... especially with my health, to get anything close to a life. Those blokes never did me any favours."

"Yes, they did! You're living safely under their roof!"

"Ronny's roof."

"Yes, okay...... Ronny's roof *now,* but don't you see? The Myton brothers have long since departed this world, so someone else has to own it. It could've been bought by someone, who not realising its history or significance, tore the place down, disposed of the machinery for its scrap value and waited until the time was right to redevelop the site, but that didn't happen...... Ronny bought it, and as we're here now, the wheel's come full circle."

"Maybe I can get that part, but getting all that kit back up and operational? Why? Where's the point? You know as well as I do that if the opportunity occurs and the time is right for Ronny to cash in on his investment, we'll all be down the road pretty bloody sharpish. No point. A waste of time, Ed."

"But what if we could make it profitable. Make it so it was worth his while hanging on to it?"

"How? Modern stuff is all computer controlled, fully automatic. This stuff belongs in a museum......"

"Yeah! That's my point! Have you ever been to the Black Country Living Museum?"

"Yeah. It's in Walsall, but that's like a complete village with shops, a pub, wharfs and shit, not an old workshop in Digbeth?"

"But it's places like this that supplied their need for stuff. I saw it in the archives, something about Netherton and the Dudley

Number Two Canal which is where that place is and how it was a staging post for storage and onward transportation of their products which links this place to it."

"Yes, but that doesn't mean that people would be interested in some scruffy old workshop in central Brum?"

"Makes me interested in it? It's a part of the legacy of the West Midlands powerhouse, the nineteenth century, the industrial revolution and what made England a force to be reckoned with all over the world. Fuck it Callum? I'm not going to walk away from this without a fight."

Callum sighed. "Alright. So we'll spruce the place up a bit. If nothing else it'll give the boys something to occupy their minds rather than pilfering stuff."

*****

Ronny had already given us the thumbs-up to do what we wanted, so priority number one was to get the old Bollinder up and running.

I didn't think it would be too difficult as we'd managed to do the deed with the first one even though we hadn't got a clue what we were doing.

I also thought, that all assuming we met with success, we'd clean it up and do a definitive job by polishing all the copper and brass pipework, repaint it in her old livery and whitewash the engine room. My idea was that if we managed to get the old machinery upstairs running and good enough to exhibit, the motor that powered them, an antique in its own right, should also be made to look the business, but first the task of cleaning years of grime and neglect from our new toys.

I asked Pip if he'd drive me across town so I could buy a laptop and mobile Wi-Fi. A printer I had back at home, but whether it would be compatible with whatever operating system came with the new computer, I had yet to discover, but that could wait.

We toured most of the tech outlets I knew until I settled on a system that would take the knocks. Not the cheapest, but there was one added bonus – they would throw in a digital camera for good measure.

Next was a visit to Office World to buy printer paper, ring binders, pens and a chalk board, we had to be organised and do things according to a plan rather than haphazardly going at it bull at a gate.

Before we went back, we stopped off at a motor factors and bought twenty-five litres of Genkleen, a concentrated and powerful degreaser, massive rolls of paper wipes, a box of industrial protective gloves and face masks.

My bank account had taken a serious hit so this venture better work, but I countered my apprehension by telling myself that if nothing else, it might just keep us occupied.

*****

Back at Bishops Wharf, the lads had been busy sweeping up the layers of crap in the workshop. They'd used an old watering can to damp the floor then working together, swept the area before loading it into buckets, lowering them out of an open window and chucking their contents into the canal.

Not good practice but what the hell!

The task that lay ahead was daunting as at every turn, more problems were unearthed such as all the electrics in that part of the building had to be ripped out and replaced. The stairs were bloody lethal, and even though I'm no engineer and not familiar with health and safety regulations, all the drives to the machinery would have to be guarded, the floor treated with non-slip paint, reinstate the fire escape and install smoke alarms and whatever else.

This was going to take rather more than the five grand I had in my account...... considerably more, but then one evening and Storytime over, a group of us were sitting around one of the fires when Mitch stuck his ore in.

"Grants. Can't you get grants for this sort of thing?"

"Possibly, but we don't own the place, and even if we did, we're still kids so nobody would take us seriously."

"Okay, but Ronny's no kid? He owns the joint, so he applies!"

"He's not interested. We have his okay to do what we want but he doesn't want to get involved."

"No damage done by asking him? The lads are having a great time cleaning the place up. None of them have been arrested in weeks, and why? Because they have something else to do, something that keeps them together and out of trouble."

"Alright. I'll talk to him, but don't run away with the idea that he'll work a minor miracle here."

*****

"Still not interested, Ed, but there's nothing to stop you from going ahead if that's what you want to do?"

"But you own the building and everything inside, not us, so how could we?"

"Right then. First off, it's not up for sale. I had hoped that after the redevelopment at Brindley Place and Gas Street Basin, the same thing might be done around here, but instead they built massive office buildings that almost devoured the Farmer's Bridge lock flight. The entire area is a tip, drunks, druggies and vagrants took it over meaning no one goes there out of choice, so I'm lumbered with property that's almost worthless, but what if I sold you a lease or rented it to you?"

"We could never afford it and still it would leave us with the problem of restoring the machinery, the safety stuff and electrics?"

"A quid a week rent so that's like five pence a week each, you get the kit – all set out legally and away you go. Approach the English Heritage people, the Black Country Museum and see what they come up with. If as you say, you've unearthed Myton's original workshop, I reckon the museum would be falling over themselves to help you.

They found out where the Aston factory was and went to see if they could buy it, but it had already been levelled, and what you have to remember, that was an addition to their operation, not the original. They managed to find some of the old kit but it was damaged beyond restoration so the interest is there...... all you have to do is sell the idea to them, set out your stall and trust to luck."

"Do you honestly think it's a goer then?"

"Nothing's certain in life, Ed, but if you follow a dream, who knows what'll happen.

One other thing I'd like you to ponder. I have always been plagued by young homeless kids, begging for food, stealing my cutlery and the like, but then Callum came along and slowly things began to change. He'd come along but he'd offer payment – I'd refuse, but then I'm a softy, plus he seemed like a genuine boy.

Then you arrived on the scene. A nice, polite and well-educated kid, totally out of step with street-life but with character and a determination to see things through to conclusion. You and Callum were destined to meet in my opinion. You are complete opposites yet the same if that makes any sense. You're right together, kindred spirits and then? Oh, my God? Along comes Pip! Between the three of you, it's difficult for me to see how you could fail. You, for example, see potential in things which others don't. That old generator being a very good example. Okay, so Callum noticed it, tried to get it to run although he didn't have a clue what it did or indeed, what it was there for, but his strength is his ability to carry the other boys along on a tide of enthusiasm, means you have a group who are happy to work alongside each other.

The other thing for you to take into consideration is, he's the one who kept you from going crazy. You're not, and never will be suited to street life, so just be thankful you took refuge where you did, found a lad who hasn't got a bad or malicious bone in his body to take care of you. Sure, he loves you, but that wasn't something that happened immediately. Most people who live rough and had found themselves a place to bed down each night, tend not to like others muscling in on their space. The love thing happened over time and you owe him a debt of thanks. Pip has the guile and tenacity to find ways around problems, sometimes not what you might call legal and above board I grant you, but then sometimes the end justifies the means. He's the fixer, the procurement man, the scammer and he's bloody good at it!

I'm making a meal of all of this, but the bottom line? You have a good little team around you. If any of my tenants realise you're here then no one has said anything, and that's because you all behave yourselves, keep your heads down and so on.

If you come up with the goods regarding that old workshop, then I won't be surprised, but before you go talking to the Black Country Museum, make inroads into the clearing up and degreasing the machinery, so if they visit, they'll understand your enthusiasm and determination to move ahead."

*****

"Grub up people. Ronny overdid things with the roast lamb dinners so I towed them back for us. Dig in before they spoil."

Buba, still working at the café seemed bullish and in a good mood.

I quizzed him over dinner.

"Ahh, well, you see. Ronny wants to slow down so he promoted me to deputy manager. He works the early shift like six in the morning 'til midday then leaves me to carry on 'til seven in the evening when the night girls arrive. The other thing? He gave me a hike in pay so now I earn more than the living wage – he even opened a bank account for me, I mean bloody-hel,l Ed? Buba Samuels with a bleedin' bank account? Next thing you'll know is, I'll be respectable!"

"Good for you, pal. You look the business in those chef's whites for sure, but respectable? Yeah, okay. Why not!"

"That's all about health and hygiene – gotta learn about all that shit as well, but like I said, I like what I do so no worries, right?"

"Go for it! I can see it now. 'Ronny's Place.' A five star Michelin restaurant!"

"Yeah, right!"

"Well, okay? Maybe not, but this lamb is to die for."

"Thank you. All my own work right down to the sauce which I reckon is a bit special."

*****

Plates cleared, and with nothing left over to chuck away and the washing-up done, we settled in for story-time but with the kids taking turns to read out loud.

They were learning fast.

Following that and before we all bedded down for the night, Callum divided the lads into work parties with one group concentrating on cleaning up the Bollinder, another working on the machinery with the rest cleaning the years of grime off the windows and preparing the walls for painting. No one was forced into helping, so if they wanted to go out into town, then fine, but it would appear that Ronny was right, as everyone nodded their willingness to pitch in.

By ten in the evening tiredness overtook, so Mitch went through and killed the generator leaving only the glow from the two fireplaces to illuminate the place. The harsh winter weather was slowly giving way to milder conditions. Spring was just around the corner, and somehow that fact alone lifted my spirits.

I cuddled tight in to Callum, kissed the nape of his neck then whispered into his ear.

"I love you."

"And I love you too, but please don't jump me tonight 'cos I'm beat!"

"Another time perhaps?"

"Deffo another time. Sleep tight, Ed. Everything is going to be fine."

Chapter Fifteen.

The weeks that followed found most of the lads getting on with the cleaning up of the machinery, engine and both the upper floor area and our squat. They had divided themselves into groups, each group responsible for a particular task and it was difficult to say which task was the most impressive.

The squat had been cleaned and two coats of white emulsion applied to the walls which lightened the interior. It did give it a clinical look, but without any direct light from outside, any other colour wouldn't be practical, and anyway, we had inherited the emulsion from the Waterways people which saved us from spending money.

The Bollinder was getting a thorough going-over. The build-up of years of grime, cobwebs and grease had been removed and items such as the cooling water tank, the fuel tank and air intake were painted with dark green Hammerite to preserve them, and the area surrounding the engine was also treated to coats of white emulsion.

The plan was that once we knew it ran, we'd polish all the brass work and paint the engine block, however that could wait.

The machinery upstairs was carefully cleaned but with everyone under strict instructions not to disturb the carriages or spindles for fear of damaging the guideways. We could take advice as to the best way to proceed later, but for me, the best bit was being able to look out of clean windows onto the wharf and the canal below. I could easily imagine working boats plying their way up and down the cut in days past. The busy wharfs, a hive of activity in the cradle of Britain's industrial revolution, although now they were just decaying relics – a sad tribute to the past.

*****

"You should come and take a gander at what Mitch has uncovered, Ed. He took a break from painting the squat and decided to see if he could pick the lock on that door in the out-building. He failed miserably so he lost his temper and smacked it with a hammer! That did the job as the lock just fell to pieces, but you ought to see what was behind that door."

"Good news or bad?"

"Dunno really. Personally, I couldn't give a fuck one way or the other, but you're so into all this historical shit you might just find your mind being blown. Oh yeah…… and bring your camera with you."

*****

We had researched Myton together with Bishops Wharf as well as we were able through the archives in the library, and all that we managed to come up with was the history of the company together with details of its past trading history, but then I remembered that they used a fleet of boats to transfer their products to Dudley and to that end, they had a wet dock at Bishops Wharf so they could load their cargo. Why they needed a wet dock given the almost two-hundred-foot frontage to the canal wasn't clear, but I followed Tiny down to the shed – camera in hand.

Mitch was standing outside looking a touch shame-faced. "Sorry, Ed, my curiosity got the better of me, but when I couldn't pick the padlock, so did my temper, so I clouted it with a hammer."

"No harm done, but please don't go hitting anything else, you might be trashing something important or valuable."

"Got it. Come see what we found inside."

For reasons still unknown, I ignored the obvious shape in the centre of the workshop covered in a rotting tarpaulin, concentrating on the collection of tools and boxes of bits and pieces that littered the benches. There were lockers containing paint tins, brushes and thinners together with boxes of rivets, nuts and bolts all sporting the manufacturers name 'Myton Fixings Limited'.

For me this was pay-dirt – the connection between the machine room and the finished product, the building I now called home and the people who once worked here.

I was snapped back to the here-and-now by Mitch who waved in the direction of the tarpaulin.

"Here's the best bit. There's a fucking boat under there!"

"A boat? What sort of boat?"

"A canal barge-type boat. Old but new, as I don't reckon it's ever seen the water. Someone was building it but maybe gave it up as a bad job and left it here. Wanna take a look?"

Mitch unsuccessfully tried to roll up the tarp but it disintegrated, but what was underneath was the shell of an old work boat. Its hull had been blacked but this was peeling away giving up the fight to surface rust. The insides of the hull had faired rather better having been painted in layers of red oxide with another tarpaulin covering the interior across the gunwales.

Further back was a deckhouse painted in a red and green livery, faded but otherwise in decent enough condition.

I eyed the plank that gave access to the stern of the boat from the dock, but it was rotten and I wasn't about to trust my luck to it, so I settled with taking photos from every angle before leaving.

"Nice find, Mitch. Don't go telling anyone outside of the squat about this, okay?"

"Don't worry. I won't say a word. Do you reckon it's important then?"

"I don't know. A boat's a boat so far as I'm concerned but it has to have some historical interest, so I'm going to pay the Black Country Museum a visit if I can get Pip to drive me there. They should be able to shed some light on this place and its significance. Why not come with me?"

*****

The next afternoon Pip took Callum, Mitch and me to Dudley and the chance to get answers to our many questions, and to begin with, the museum's secretary didn't seem too keen on disturbing the curator over some casual enquiry from a bunch of scruffy kids, but I turned on my Grammar School voice and eventually we did manage to see him.

"Myton you say? Yes, I know of the company. They manufactured fastenings for the ship and boat building industry and latterly, they supplied BSA during the two world wars. They closed their doors to production in 1947 and the Myton brothers retired to the country and their workshop abandoned and later sold for redevelopment.

What is your interest here?"

"They closed for business, that's true enough, and the Aston plant is no more, but what of their facility in Digbeth?"

"I imagine it went before Aston as Digbeth was their original factory. Our understanding was that all production was moved from there between the wars."

"Not so. Take a look at these photos. These were taken two days ago. Maybe production moved, but their original workshops still exist together with machinery and their old wet-dock. There's more – much more, but this is just to give you an idea of what we've uncovered so far."

He leafed through the photos then I handed him the catalogue we'd found.

"We've boxes of rivets, nuts, bolts, washers and stuff we can't identify – all packed in their original containers. The workshop houses some very old machinery together with cutting tools and half-finished items, almost as if they left in a hurry. We've already managed to get their electricity generator running, and now we've found the engine that drove the machines, and with luck, it shouldn't be too long before that's up and running as well."

"Fascinating, but if you're looking to sell, it's pretty much worthless."

"We understand that, but historically, it has to be significant doesn't it?"

"Significant yes. Unfortunately, many old factories were razed to the ground with the demolition people completely unaware of what they were looking at, but we can't realistically go uprooting a factory and relocating it here? It's just not feasible."

"And also its significance to Digbeth would be lost."

"Yes. Location is everything with things like this. Could I see it?"

"Yes please. I hold the lease and we'd appreciate some advice in its restoration and upkeep."

"The building?"

"Yes, I lease it but I own the contents to do with as I see fit, and my *See Fit* is to restore it. The building isn't my responsibility."

"Okay. So when would it be convenient to visit you?"

"Whenever suits you. Just don't expect to find a nice, organised place. We're doing our best, but funds; well they're somewhat limited let's just say."

"As is the case with all industrial heritage projects. This museum took years of planning, fighting the local authorities and so on. All of us who were involved from the outset, did what we did during our spare time with none of us being paid; not even expenses, so I know the score.

If we can agree on two tomorrow afternoon, then I'll bring a couple of engineering experts with me. They should be able to give you some information and guidance regarding the workshop and how best to preserve it. I'll come armed with video equipment and still cameras so we can document everything."

"Good enough, although we don't want any of this to become public knowledge; at least, not now."

"That's a given. Two tomorrow afternoon then?"

*****

"Was that such a good idea Ed? They know where we are and what we've got, and that makes me nervous."

"Listen up Callum? They're just a bunch of enthusiasts who bury their noses in the past; boffins and eccentrics. They're not interested in us, just what we've uncovered.

Doubtless they've come across kit similar to what's in the workshop before, and it isn't valuable, however what *is* valuable isn't so much what we have, but where it is; everything we've found was untouched since the Myton brothers chose to take retirement so making it like a time capsule, a snapshot to a forgotten era. They restore back-to-back terrace houses now, the likes of which even the rats have moved out of. The past is seen as important – an asset, and an example of how things used to be and perhaps it'll stop people from thinking that their lives are like so much shit – make them realise just how much things have changed for the better instead of carping on about how much the world owes them a living."

"You're wrong on so many fucking levels! What the fuck do you know about life on the street and the reasons behind why people believe it's the only escape from their problems. You know about Pip – you know about me, but we're on the lighter side of things. You've no idea about what drives kids onto the streets and away from their families. It's every young person's idea of a nightmare but still they do it. Life *IS SHIT for them* but they see an escape from whatever was tormenting them by living rough, and no fucking museum is going to change Jack Shit!"

Pip drew the car to a halt and threw me a look which basically told me to shut up.

"I don't believe that Ed was trying to preach to us. Sure, he isn't aware of the abuse and shit that a lot of the kids have been subjected to, but that's a plus in my book.

Be reasonable Callum? Look at the guy who you love and accept the fact that at the very least he's trying to make a difference despite his lack of understanding? The Farmers Lock Flight crew are lost causes because no one was bothered to listen, but our lot? They came to be with us when the weather turned cold, but it's June in just under a week and most of them are still with us. What does that tell you?"

"Tells me that they've found an easy option. Regular hot food, a cosy and dry place to crash, and all for helping clean up a heap of shit Ed thinks is important. Their enthusiasm will disappear as will they. There's no hope for any of them."

"What's eating at you Callum? Think back to when you two met up. What's changed and how do you feel about it?"

Callum put his head in his hands and thought about Pip's comments before turning to me.

"Sorry, Ed. That was uncalled for and I apologise. I don't get all this history bollocks, but the boys are animated and if it helps them to learn shit, then who am I to go throwing stones."

"I'm not looking for apologies and I'll go with that perhaps my approach was wrong, but all I wanted was to fire their enthusiasm for something other than stealing another wallet, nicking another car or breaking into another house. Just to see that there can be other ways to go. I'm not a social worker or a shrink; I don't know how to deal with abused and frightened kids? All I'm trying to do is occupy their minds doing something passably enjoyable.

Look at the squat. They clean up after themselves and take pride in their surroundings. This seems to have carried over to the old workshop. They feel like they own it and need to clean it up. The other day, one of the younger boys came down stairs and almost begged me to follow him so he could show me the name plate he'd found on one of the lathes. No big deal, right? But for him it was like the discovery of a lifetime. He asked me to read it to him but I refused and had *him* read it. He managed it pretty well, and here's a boy who couldn't write his own name three months ago? Even if they buggered off tomorrow – which they won't, at least we've managed to sow seeds which might germinate into positive actions in the future."

"So it's not about you scratching an itch, but more like a means to an end?"

"Yeah. Just like that. While they're here they work as a team rather than doing their own thing. They might leave us, but I hope they don't."

Pip, who had remained silent throughout this exchange of words, decided to speak up.

"You have to admit that Ed has a point. Look at Buba as a prime example. I know what shit he had to deal with as a young boy, but look at him now? He's gone from that big jovial oaf to getting a job washing plates at Ronny's, to a short order chef to shift supervisor and all in a matter of months.

Yeah, okay. Ronny's isn't like your swanky five-star establishment, but it's paid employment. Buba pays National Insurance and income tax – he has a track record that could take him onwards to better things and all 'cos he came here when it was too cold to doss the streets."

"I know and I'm sorry, but I've shit of my own to deal with – heavy, heavy shit."

"Do you wanna talk about it?"

"I dunno. What's going down scares me and a part of me doesn't want to involve anyone else, but then again, I feel the need to let it all out. If I go telling anyone, it won't just be me looking down the barrel of a gun or worse, it'll be their arses in a sling as well. It's too much of a risk, Pip."

"We've managed to work through stuff in the past, so why not now?"

"Because this goes beyond scamming, that's why. Yes, we've blagged our way out of some nasty situations before, but this is different. Ask yourselves a question. Do I normally look like someone frightened of their own shadow? Do you see me as a kid who's scared to go into town or frightened to walk the streets at night? No. I'll bet not, but...... I fucking-well am now!"

I'd never seen this side of Callum before. He had moods sometimes; I think all of us did, but I was looking at a kid – yeah a kid – scared half to death, and no matter what, he had to tell us what was frightening him so much.

"Please, Callum? I know you're trying to protect us, but if you don't confide in someone; and who better than those who love you, you'll go into meltdown. There's no need to name names, but to get a handle on what this is all about might give us ideas?"

"You'd put your head in a noose for me?"

"Yeah. Why not! You saved me from turning myself in to the authorities or risk freezing to death so now it's payback time for me, the others can choose how they play it for themselves."

Mitch went with me with Pip hot on his heels.

We pulled over into a layby to talk.

Chapter Sixteen.

"I hope this pissing vehicle is road legal?"

"Relax, Callum. Taxed, tested and insured only last month. The law, if they decide to give us the once-over, won't find anything unless you're smoking weed in that ciggie."

"Weed? I don't even touch *alcohol!*"

"So, what gives, and don't try to duck out of this or you'll find yourself using Shank's Pony to get back to Digbeth, and going down the Soho Road in Handsworth ain't a nice place to be."

Callum thought before looking at us, but the warning about the prospect of walking through one of the less welcoming areas of Birmingham loosened his tongue.

"You know I used to be on the rent. I preferred to call myself a Demolition Operative 'cos I destroyed erections pretty bloody quickly. I was cute, and my body turned men of a certain kind into gibbering idiots and most times they'd pop their cork before even touching me. Sometimes I had to Perform, and that sickened me, but it was all about survival and getting through the day, so I did what I had to do. I could net myself, - fifty quid, may be tops one hundred a night, but sometimes if the weather was crap, I wouldn't turn a trick, so living was hand-to-mouth; that was until I met up with this bloke who just gave me a mobile phone and a fistful of cash for doing fuck-all, telling me to call the only number stored in its memory before fucking off.

Five hundred notes and a mobile, and I never had to get my kit off? I called this number the next morning."

"And?"

"Parties. They held sex romps for perverts. They wanted me to be one of their little boys so the customers could get their rocks off doing anything they wanted to me."

Pip put his head in his hands and collapsed onto the steering wheel.

"Oh God. I've heard about that sort of thing and some kids don't live to tell the tale."

"Shit like that isn't like an everyday thing, but you're right, it happens.

Thing was, I was looked upon as something that bit special. A young Oriental boy who was a natural bottom, cute-looking, smooth and completely hairless...... I was a prized possession for the bloke who ran this caper. He saw me as his meal ticket plus fuck loads more so no way was he about to have me snuffed...... unless the price was right."

By this time, I was also getting to the point where I wanted to throw-up but I persevered enough to keep Callum on track.

"Look. I'm not going to ask what exactly you had to do, but give us a break here? You're telling us that he, whoever he was, was willing to sacrifice you?"

"There's a price for everything, and if you have the dosh then you can buy and sell pretty much whatever you like, and if you are sadistic enough to want to kill a kid while forcing him or her to perform whatever sex acts necessary, then there'll always be people around who are in a position to provide that service, and also, clear up the mess afterwards."

"So you were......"

"Up for sale. Highest bidder takes all...... in this case, my life with no come-backs. £200000, more if the buyer wanted it put on video, more again if he wanted an audience. A simple strangulation is at the going rate, but if there's blood, they pay a premium for the clear-up. Bodies are stuffed into a lime pit on a farm, and give it a few weeks...... no evidence. Another street kid gone with no one giving a toss, so no police – no problem."

I threw open the car door and vomited into the gutter, retching my guts up until there wasn't anything else to give. Memories of earlier conversations about Callum's lifestyle just served to prove how naïve I was, how depraved humanity could be, even in England.

It took Pip to calm me down, or at least, try to put some perspective on things.

"This is our problem, Ed. None of us know what's a good deal or what's bad. We're lowlife and there are people who'll take advantage of us knowing there's fuck-all we can do about it. We can't allow ourselves to trust anyone; the police are corrupt – a lot of the time they're in the pockets of criminals, and people who appear to be charity workers might be on the lookout for vulnerable kids to sell on for whatever needs are out there.

Take your copper as an example. On paper, he seemed okay, but have you heard from him since handing over that charge card? How can you be sure he didn't go straight to the bank and pocket the lot? You can't, so now do you understand? He might've been one of the good guys, but then, if there were no records of the conversations you had with him, and with that Vincent bloke out of the picture, and your Mum...... sorry, but do you see what I'm trying to tell you? If he was bent, he could just take the money and fuck off with no one the wiser."

"Yes, I hear you. Where do we go from here? You talked about heavy stuff going down, but that part of your life is over isn't it, Callum?"

"Over yes, but not forgotten, either by me or the arsehole who ran the operation. Word is, he's looking for me, and if he finds me? I don't think you need brains to figure out that he doesn't just want to say Hi. I'm a loose cannon and he'll only be safe once I'm tied down and put out of action."

"Why? How can he know that you know this client of his was looking to snuff you?"

"They sedated the kids to make absolutely sure they co-operated. They were like zombies, but I have a tolerance to that shit, and once he'd finished with me, I overheard that conversation about being taken out. I was taken back into town – everything cool, but I switched the phone off and went to ground, and to be honest, I didn't really think about it until that drug thing and the charge card."

"What's that got to do with child prostitution!"

"Nothing. But do you remember finding that phone and listening to that voicemail? Vincent being a very naughty boy and how he'd end up propping up a motorway bridge somewhere if he didn't cough up the cash? I recognised that voice. It was Carl's voice, the guy who hosted those parties."

"So, he's into trafficking drugs *and* child prostitution, but that's no proof he's looking for you?"

"There's been words on the street. He's looking for me alright, but the bit that scared the crap out of me was this afternoon at the museum.

Did you notice a photo on the wall of this curator's office? A bloke and about four kids making it look like a family photo?"

"Yes, I saw it. What of it?"

"The man in the picture was Carl, and one of the boys was me. That's What of It, Ed! This curator bloke is a fucking pervert and was one of the fuckers who attended the parties. I noticed him staring at me, he recognised me, Ed, and you fucking-well told the bastard where to find us!"

*****

"Solihull *NOW, and fuck the speed limits! Just GO!"*

"*Solihull? You're having a laugh right?"*

"No one knows you there – you'll be out of harm's way."

"Oh, yeah, okay. 'My name is Edward Anderson.' Your mother shacked up with a guy who fucked off with a tidy fortune that was due to Carl, lived at your place for God knows how long, and you're telling me Carl's not about to go adding up the sums? I'm safer in Digbeth!"

"Alright. Dumb idea. Where else is there?"

Mitch, who had remained quiet throughout, spoke up.

"The boat I uncovered. See if it floats, and if it's sound enough, Callum could doss on that. You never mentioned it at the museum, so it's like our secret hideaway."

"Yeah, but it's in the shed and anyone might go poking around."

"Not if it floats, they won't. There's a mooring behind Ronny's joint, so if we parked it there? Who's to suspect?"

"It might work but it isn't very welcoming."

Callum giggled for the first time that afternoon. "I've been in worse places! Who else knows about this boat Mitch?"

"No one so far as I know. I told Tiny about me trashing the padlock, but never said anything about what was inside apart from it might be interesting to you."

"That's something at least. I don't mind disappearing for a bit, but how will we know when it's safe for me to come home? A few nights – a few weeks is fine, but I do have a life."

Pip got out of the car and stretched himself before getting back behind the wheel and starting the engine.

"Impossible to say. I'm thinking of ways we can turn the tide on him; make it him that has plenty to worry about rather than us. Where did he operate out of?"

"If you're talking about where he held those parties, then it was some up-market pad in leafy Warwickshire. I don't know the name of the village; they gave me a shot of something as soon as I got into their car plus I had to wear a blindfold, but like I told you, I have a tolerance to the stuff, so it was easy to dislodge the blindfold, pretend to be totally out of it and watch the route they took. Get us onto the A45 out of town towards Coventry, and I'd probably be able to figure out where we went."

"Well, it's all we have to go on, so let's see if your memory is up to the task."

*****

"No, sorry. It was that turn back there. The one on the left just after that pub."

"Good thing we've got a full tank of fuel or we'd be in Shit Street!"

"I can't help it? I was drugged and obviously didn't have my wits about me."

"Never mind. Do we have much further to go?"

"No. We're close now; at least I think we are, but I'm a townie, not a fucking sheep-shagger so all these hedgerows look the same to me!"

*****

"Upper Wootton Magna. Mean anything to you?"

"Hey! Wootton Park. That's the name of the house!"

"Don't get too excited Callum. We've still got to find the place."

"Can't miss it. Fuck-off massive iron gates; locked of course. The driver had like a button he pressed that opened the gates then closed them once we were through. Then there's this long drive through a wood before reaching the house."

"Sounds as if your pal Carl was doing okay for himself!"

"I reckon."

*****

"Hey guys? Now this is what I call a pad, and it's up for sale!"

"Yeah. Nice enough house if you like the idea of wandering around empty hallways at night, paying for all the electric, gas and heating for something around half the size of Buckingham Palace with no nice big family to share it with. Fuck that!"

"We're going to take a look around though right? We can't come all this way just to look at a pair of gates; what we need is something to swing at this Carl bloke, and standing around outside ain't gonna get us anywhere."

"I just know I'm going to rue the day I agreed to this. C'mon, what's the hold up?"

The gates, being secure, meant we had to find another way to access the property, but we persevered finding a gap between the fence that spanned a dry ditch, so now it was Game On and a very risky trespass onto someone's private land.

I'm sure I wasn't alone in looking out for CCTV cameras or other bits and pieces of stuff that might suggest surveillance, but the wood we walked through almost seemed inviting with trail tracks clearly signposted like a trim-trail or a more-gentle nature walk, but the neglect we saw as we came to the edge of the tree line spoke of a property uncared for and left to nature. The once well-tended lawns were overgrown and a haven for meadow flowers and butterflies, the formal gardens were untended and sad; the driveway had weeds growing up through the tarmac, and I doubted this house had been occupied for at least a year if not more. There were internal shutters at the windows, and again looking for security cameras but finding nothing obvious, we skirted around this very impressive building and first took a look at the extensive outbuildings which included a garage block containing three black Range Rover 4.6 litre Sport SUV's each with keys in the ignitions.

"Not very security-conscious, this Carl?"

"Yeah, well, would your common thief run the risk of getting past locked gates, a half-mile trek to an old house on the off-chance he might find a vehicle decent enough to nick, Ed?"

"I suppose not."

"But it does give us an exit strategy if we're sussed, so no wandering off okay? We keep together at all times."

"So you think there's someone else here?"

"Who knows, but it's always sensible to plan for the unexpec-ted, and for us to get split up for whatever reason is a bum idea."

Callum awoke from his trance. "Those are the vehicles they used to collect the kids, and he probably thought it was too much of a risk to have them out cruising the streets. The number plates are most likely duds anyway.

If there is anyone here, we can easily tell as there are only three ways into the house. One at the front, one at the back and another on the side of the building which leads into the old ser-vant's quarters. They put bars across the doors to stop people from getting in, so if the place is empty, all the bars will be in place as you can't fit them from the inside."

"So, we won't be able to get inside either. Great!"

Pip grinned. "Where there's will, there's a way boyo."

*****

Having circled the house and finding all the doors very se-curely blocked off, we went for another sortie.

All the ground floor windows had security locks fitted on the inside plus they had steel bars bolted to the walls with the screw heads filed away so they would be a pig to remove even if you had the time to give it a go.

Uninvited guests obviously not encouraged at Wootton Park.

We met with more success at the rear of the property. I found a set of two trapdoors angled out of the wall at about forty-five degrees, and they weren't locked.

On opening them, we looked down into a cellar which housed empty beer barrels and cases of various spirits together with a well-stocked wine rack. We listened carefully for any noises, and on hearing nothing, we lowered ourselves down and onto the floor below. Callum found a light switch and switching it on, a line of bare bulbs on ceiling roses flicked into life.

Pip took a closer look at one of these that had failed to light up.

"Fifty volt and battery powered which means there has to be a generator somewhere. Find that and we've solved another mystery."

We found it lurking away behind a door on which was pinned a notice. "Authorised Personnel Only. High Voltage." We took a look purely out of interest. The manufacturer's label indicated a maximum output of 250 kV at 415 volts AC. I traced the output feeder cable to a huge inverter and a separate industrial battery bank and charging equipment labelled "50 Volt DC at 10.000 kW. Extreme Danger to Life."

"Okay then. Let's see if we can get access to the house from in here, shall we?"

We carefully retraced our steps back to where we had managed to get in and took a look around. A pair of doors directly in front of the pile of barrels looked as if they might be promising, but naturally they were locked, but then Pip took out a pen torch and peered through the keyhole.

"Eureka! They left the key in the lock! How bloody careless can you get. Find something like a thin piece of cardboard and a bit of wire and I'll net the thing."

Cardboard we had bucket loads of, but wire posed a problem until I went back to the generator room where I found a reel of the stuff beside the bank of batteries, and ten long minutes later, Pip had teased the key from the lock where it fell onto the slip of cardboard he'd run under the door and gently pulling it back underneath, we had ourselves a key, but before we could use it, we heard the distant chatter of helicopter rotors.

"Cut the lights, get the fuck out and shut the doors. Time we left I reckon."

One by one we scrambled through the trap doors, closed them behind us and looked for cover between the garage block and the many other outbuildings grouped around the area. Safe enough for now, but with Pip having taken it upon himself to lead us out of trouble, we followed him closely as the 'copter swung in a broad arc before coming to land on the front lawn. The pilot kept the powerful searchlight switch on and the rotors turning as if the occupants ere nervous about something, but then another SUV, not a Range Rover, but an ML Series Mercedes Benz 4x4 tore up the drive, turned facing the way it came in and the two occupants stepped out of the vehicle and waited until the helicopter's motors were silenced and two more men appeared. The pilot was dressed in a flashy Bermuda short sleeved shirt and cut-offs, his passenger sporting a lounge suit, collar and tie similar to the two guys from the SUV.

Callum gasped. "Fucking hell. The Main Man and his three wise monkeys. The twat with the shirt is Carl, the other three are his henchmen, but importantly, the guy who arrived with Carl is the same guy who recruited me. Nice enough on the surface, but one nasty bastard otherwise. We tread very carefully around them."

Pip turned to him. "I'm not about to stick around long enough to find out how mean or otherwise they might be. We need out of here, and right now."

"Oh, yeah? And how do you propose scamming that trick? Can you fly a chopper? We can't just walk out of here all casual-like? "Nice place you got mate! Shame about not cutting the grass? Get real, Pip!"

"I'm not about to take up flying, but what I can do a passably good job at is *driving!* That beast in front of us is an ML 65 AMG All Terrain 4x4, and for my money, the best of the best. A fuck--off massive 6.5 litre V8 with a drive pack to trash anything currently on the market, so we nick it, bugger up the chopper and do a runner. They'll have to fire up one of the Range Rovers in the garage before they can think about chasing after us, and by the time they've got over the shock of being had, we're in the Astra and long gone."

"You're a fucking headcase. Do you know that?"

"Quite possibly. Have you anything better to add to the mix? If not, just shut the fuck up and do what I say when I say it. I'm going try to get over to the vehicle unnoticed, but if it goes tits, you're on your own, but if I manage it okay, then I'll wave you and you can come and join me. Hopefully Braindead left keys in the ignition and we're home and gone, otherwise we leg it through the woods. Any questions?"

*****

Pip crept along by the wall nearest to the garage then paused, almost unsure what to do next, but then he stood up and took a look around before rolling up his sleeve to the elbow and shattered a pane of glass in the window. He paused again, then satisfied it hadn't been heard from the house, popped the latch and let himself in emerging moments later, waving three sets of keys at us before pocketing them.

Still no movement from the house, he sprinted over to the Mercedes and took a look inside. A wave from him and we followed, running towards the car, and with still no movement from the house, we climbed in to the back seats as Pip started the engine.

"Strap yourselves in and hold on to your hats. I'm going to try and hit the rear rotor on the 'copter, but if I miss it, then I'll smack the nose cone which should bugger its aerodynamics enough to make it difficult to get off the ground."

He hit a switch that, as he explained later, disabled the traction control or on older 4x4's, effectively served to lock the differential gearboxes enabling all four wheels to rotate at the same speed giving much needed grip across the damp grass. He gunned the accelerator and the Merc took off like a rocket, slithered across the grass before digging itself in and hurtled towards the back of the helicopter. It hit the rear rotor with a thump which was hard enough to lift the offside wheels of the car off the ground and Pip momentarily losing control. The Merc slewed around before he managed to regain steerage then went for the nose cone, clipping it sufficiently enough to rip off some panels.

"Let's get out of here and now! That had to be heard miles away."

"Gate. What about the gates? They'll be locked shut. Any sign of an activator?"

Pip ran his fingers behind the sun visor. "Nothing here. He must've put it in his pocket."

"So how do we get out?"

"Ram the gates and hope this baby has the power to bust through them. From here on, I don't have a game plan, but if we break through, we get back to the Astra, you guys get into the boot and leave the rest to me."

Chapter Seventeen.

"Hands behind your heads and heads between your knees; we're going through those gates, so brace yourselves!"

Oh man, did we ever hit the gates, but then the noise of the car's body panels tearing to pieces was overtaken by the ML's powerful brakes locking all four wheels as it shot across the lane before nose-diving into a ditch. The bull-bars bent backwards shattering the radiator grill and pushing the three twelve-inch cooling fans into the radiator, shredding it and sending clouds of steam skywards.

"Nice one Pip. Remind me not to let you test drive anything else I might buy."

"Needs Must as they say, but now, and if you're up for it, it's back to the Astra so I can think about our next move."

*****

"I'm thirsty and I could use something to eat, so I'm going to nip over to the shop and get something. Want anything while I'm there?"

"Mineral water and a sandwich sounds good, but shouldn't we be on our way?"

"Not just yet. I wanna leave it a bit then go and see what's happening, but that means you two having to cuddle up in the boot for a while."

"Huh? Why do we have to do that?"

"'Cos I'm the only one that no one knows. Callum...... well enough said, but you, Ed, you were at the front of that presentation to the museum about our place, but I parked up in a busy public car park and stayed behind. No one will recognise me and anyway, I'm job hunting!"

"You're a nutter. A serious fucking headcase!"

"Callum, my mate? Watch this space and be amazed!"

Pip managed to get some of those pre-packed sandwiches that looked as if they contained something, but actually, what there was, was just a glob of filling in the centre; oh, and chilled mineral water, but it's mightily difficult drinking anything when you're flat on your back in a confined space.

Pip hung around for about fifteen minutes before starting the car and making his way down the road, but then he stopped and we could hear talking.

"Bloody-hell, mate? That looks serious. What happened and is there anything I can do to help?"

"A momentary lapse in concentration, but no, there's nothing you can do, but thanks for asking."

"You don't need a lift anywhere then?"

"No ta. I've managed to organise the recovery people and I can get a lift with them. Ah *SHIT!* My missus will shred my arse for this! I only collected it yesterday – it was supposed to be a wedding anniversary present to her."

"You must love her very much! An ML 65 AMG. The dog's bits when it comes to all terrain kit."

"You know a lot about cars then?"

"I know what I like, but then I also know what I can afford, if you see what I mean!"

"Nothing wrong with Vauxhalls. My first car was a beaten up old Nova but it got me from A to B for about three years, and even then I managed to sell it on afterwards.

You come across as an intelligent kid? What's your line of work?"

"Not long left school, so it's Agricultural College for me come September. I wanna be a farmer."

"Have you managed to find holiday work?"

"Oh, yeah, if you fancy stacking shelves in a Supermarket or crappy zero-hours contract work which net you next to sod-all, otherwise nothing I fancy doing. My folks aren't made of money, so I'll have to find myself something that gives me hours, and also, something I can get my teeth into."

"Gardening perhaps?"

"I can do that, but it'd have to be a big spread. I work hard and I need the hours, so a tiddly back garden isn't what I'm after."

"Can you get here for Saturday afternoon, say around one o'clock? Come up to the house behind the gates that've been trashed. I have gardens that would keep an army occupied, and I'll cough up the money if you prove your worth."

"You've got it! What's your name?"

"Carl. Carl Mitchel, and yours?"

"Peter Standish – Pete or Pip to my friends."

"Well then, Pete Standish? I'll look forward to seeing you on Saturday."

*****

Pip didn't let us out of the boot until we were miles away from Wootton Magna, and even then he told us to keep our heads down. He was playing a very dangerous game, but he was his old confident self when at last we were set free to stretch our legs.

"What are you at Pip? You're inviting yourself into the lion's enclosure here!"

"That's not how I see it. You saw the state of the grounds, and if he has plans to open the place up for...... whatever, he has to smarten the place up, and I'm going to be the one who does it."

"Yeah, but......"

"Yeah, but what, Callum? I gain his trust by working my nuts off, he in return, gives me extra responsibilities until he allows me access to the house. All sorted. It isn't going to happen overnight, but as we discovered this afternoon, it's not a good idea to go poking around without permission so you'll have to be patient."

"I still don't like it. What if he tries to get you to...... you know?"

"Look at me? I have problems getting my rocks off whatever the situation. I'm skinny, my hair refuses to co-operate, I'm getting zits where I really don't need them? What bloke, no matter how perverted he is, is going to take a shine to me!"

"Have it your own way, but it still leaves us with the problem of where to tuck Callum away and out of sight before we get a visit from the museum bloke. The boat idea is fine but we don't know if it'll float. It's going to take time to put it in the water, and if we hit problems, it'd be far better if we could come up with a Plan B."

"Yeah, and not only that, I'm firmly on the radar now, and if I stay around here, I'm going to get picked up eventually. I have a couple of mates down in London who might be able to put me up until this all blows over; if it ever blows over."

"Call them. See if they're willing to help then. Who out of all the lads are the most trustworthy?"

"Tiny and Mitch. I've known them since living on the streets, and apart from petty thieving, they're both straight-up guys. Why do you ask?"

"Well, given the seriousness of this situation, it might be wise to have someone else in the loop in case of trouble. If Callum gets the nod and runs south, we could tell the kids that he's gone up to Liverpool or Manchester. That way, if they get asked, they can only go telling what they think they know rather than knowing his real destination and screwing things up, but there's still safety in numbers for us if we have a couple of others on board as backup."

Callum thought for a moment. "Makes sense. I'm happy with that. If these fuckers are really looking for me, and if one of the kids is careless enough to get fingered, then it'll send Carl and his blokes searching blind alleyways"

"Phone. Does Carl have your number?"

"No. The only way he could contact me was by calling the phone I was given."

"Well, that's something at least. I suggest you cut up the SIM card and chuck the handset into the canal. You can't afford to have anything in your possession that could link you to him."

*****

By mid-evening, Callum had his answer. He was welcome to stay with his friends in London for the duration. Apparently they'd been active in helping some kids in London escape from the clutches of people-traffickers who wanted to export them to the Middle East where young blond boys are traded openly. Quite how they managed it, Callum wasn't sure, and all he said was that the person at the head of this organisation was "Put out of action." Anyway, he was going to let the commuter rush subside, then get the first available train into London the following morning.

The next item on the agenda was to get Mitch and Tiny on their own so we could explain what was going down. They mostly hung out together, so as soon as they got back, we took a walk along the towpath.

"That's it in a nutshell. So far as the other kids know, Callum is going up to either Liverpool or Manchester. That way, if they are asked, they can appear unsure of his actual destination. Only the five of us know where he's really going, so keep it tight okay? Any questions?"

Tiny spoke up. "Anything else we can do, Ed?"

"Pip and I are taking Callum to New Street Station in the morning. And it might be an idea if you came along for the ride. In the unlikely event we get sussed, we can cause a diversion and either get him out of there, or safely onto the train."

"One other thing? You should tell Buba and Ronny. Buba's been a loyal friend to you, Callum, and it might be a smart move to get an adult on side as well."

Callum smiled at this comment. "Leave that to me. You're right and I'd forgotten about Buba. Ronny's been very kind to me over the years and I reckon he'd be well pissed off if I didn't tell him."

"Who's going to tell the others?"

"No one. We just act all casual for now, but if anyone asks, we tell them our lie and let it go around like a Chinese Whisper. No point in making a big deal out of this. So Callum's gone away for a while. So fucking-what! He's free to do his own thing, isn't he?"

*****

Friday morning at New Street Station saw a sad farewell. There were no incidents, and before we finally managed to get Callum on the train, there were hugs all round, and a rather prolonged one for me. His final comment before he let go of me was a simple "Miss me, Ed. I'm in love with you."

*****

The drive back to Bishop's Wharf was at best, subdued. I knew well enough why *I* felt despondent, I was separated from Callum for the first time since doing a runner. He had become my anchor, always around to lift my spirits, but why Pip, Mitch and Tiny were downbeat was another matter. I thought about this before I spoke up.

"He's going to be fine. His mates will look out for him."

Mitch studied the floor before turning to me.

"Let's hope you're right. People like the ones he got tangled up with are like a virus. They multiply and divide, mutate and gain immunity from prosecution 'cos they buy their way in to polite and decent society. They rub shoulders with influential people and worm their way in to their confidence and gain their trust. Before you know it, their reputation of being good outstanding citizens, and coupled with generous donations to good causes, buys them protection.

Maybe even if Pip does finds something he could use against this Carl bloke, who could he take it to? Not all coppers are bent, but then they might take the view that Carl and his flamboyant and totally over-the-top generosity couldn't possibly be guilty of child molestation, not to mention being an accessory to murder? A street kid's word versus that of a pillar of the community? Just think about it, Ed?"

"That was you talking Mitch?"

"I know how to use words. Reading them, spelling them even; that's my problem."

"Well, I *have to believe* he's going to be okay or I'd go mental."

Pip turned the car into a MacDonald's car park and turned the engine off.

"Ed's right, and we have to work on the principal that Callum's safe, but then he isn't like that bigger threat to this Carl? He's small fry, and once they get their heads around the fact that Callum's left for somewhere else, even if they have contacts in other cities, they're not going to waste their time and resources looking for some kid who's running scared. Too much of a risk, a risk that might blow their operations apart if they get too nosey.

One other thing? I haven't got a fucking clue what I'm looking for. I don't know if I'll even find anything for that matter, but there's no harm done by trying. If something does turn up, then we'll have to think very carefully about how we play it. It has to be bomb-proof, whatever it is. Turning it in, and to whoever is another thing we can worry about come the time, but not right now."

"We should get back then. I'd like to pay some more attention to the boat. I need something to take my mind off all this shit, all this stuff surrounding Callum and his activities."

*****

"At least the slings held! How's it looking inside Harry?"

"Can't see any water in the cargo bit, but they laid floor planks in the cabin so I can't see fuck-all unless we take them up which by the way, ain't hard to do. They never got around to nailing them down!"

"Take one up then. If she's leaking, we'll have to lift her back out or risk losing her."

Ten long minutes later, Harry poked his head up from the supposed engine room.

"There's water getting in from where the drive shaft goes out. It's not much of a leak, and otherwise she's dry."

"There's an *engine in there?"*

"Yeah. Just like the one we use for the electric 'cept this one looks like new."

"Another motor to recommission, but this one shouldn't be too much of a hardship at least."

"Yeah, but this leak might be a problem unless you haul her out pretty quickly!"

*****

The next morning and a visit to a boat yard confirmed that the stern gland was leaking. Questions about how long it had been since the calking had been replaced wasn't something I could answer, so I bought gasket rope and grease and with some questions of my own about how to do the job, we went back to the wharf.

Two days later we were due the visit from the Curator of the Black Country Museum. I didn't want to get halfway involved in a job I had little understanding about before this meeting, so the boat stayed up in the dock and out of the water and my time was spent wondering what I could do to keep the kids away from the place whilst my visitors were here.

Actually, my worries were put to bed when Buba mentioned something about a barbeque at a local haunt he visited. One of these blokes was celebrating a minor lottery win and everyone off the streets was welcome to go along.

The day of the visit saw just me and Ronny on the premises with him as the landlord and me as the registered tenant.

Three men arrived; the one I'd met at the museum, another I didn't know, but the third I did recognise as Carl, the guy who recruited young boys for sex orgies, and my guard went up immediately.

I don't think we got off to a good start as both the curator and Carl seemed more interested in my involvement, my background and home address.

"So, Mr Woolacott, that's a West Country name, isn't it?"

"Devon born to Devon parents. Tavistock as it happens."

"What brought you to Birmingham then?"

"Family matters, and private. Why all the questions about me? I thought you'd be more interested in what I've uncovered."

"Just trying to be friendly? Your accent was more Warwickshire than Birmingham; definitely not West Country so I thought I'd ask the question."

"My family background and business has nothing whatsoever to do with why you're here; where I live and the reasons why I'm leasing this building likewise, so perhaps I could show you around?"

Disinterest was putting it mildly.

"It has an historical interest of sorts. The equipment is of no value; there must be many hundreds of abandoned workshops scattered around Birmingham and the Black Country, so really there's nothing here we'd want to buy."

"Not mine to sell even if I could. That wasn't the reason I asked you to view it. I need technical advice about how to restore it all and I thought I'd made that very clear when I came to see you."

"You'd be much better served by putting an advert in the local rag. There have to be retired engineers out there who remember this kit. In short? I cannot help you."

*****

Shortly after they'd gone, I locked up and walked with Ronny up to his café, and over a mug of tea we talked about the visit.

"I don't believe they had any intention of giving us any advice. That curator bloke saw Callum when we went to see him so I reckon it was all about finding out if he'd be here and where he was hiding out."

"Quite possibly, but what I don't understand is who was the third guy. Okay, we know the curator is tied up with this Carl fella, but what if our mystery man is also involved and in what capacity."

"Shame there's no CCTV cameras around, Callum might've recognised him."

"I could try and sketch him; I'm a pretty mean artist when I get the chance."

"That's not a bad idea. I think it might be a good thing if all the boys knew the face, maybe one of them might remember him from somewhere.

I don't like this Ronny? I never knew living on the streets could be so dangerous."

"Well, if everyone uses their heads and stays put here during the evenings and overnight, you should be safe enough. There are no windows on the front of the building and you're not overlooked from the canal, so just keep the gates secure and stay vigilant. Any problems, just give me a call. I have some heavyweight friends who owe me, and they like nothing better than to get involved in a duel."

"Comforting not!"

"No, seriously, Ed. These boys are nasty bastards. They used to run with a gang out of Aston; their thing was extortion, fraud and money laundering, but never child prostitution or abuse. They dealt very quickly and effectively with any member of their organisation that stepped over the line."

"So like your thinking man's thug then?"

"Violence wasn't their trademark, Ed. Money was the prime objective, but if anyone put their operation in jeopardy? Bye-bye, never to be heard from again.

I believe their boss called it ruthless efficiency!"

"I'm not sure I'd like to meet them!"

"Actually, you'd like them; in fact, I reckon it might be a good idea if you did meet up with them. They might prove to be a massive ally with your war with this Carl individual."

"How come? You said they weren't into violence."

"No, they're not, but they have a network of contacts – people who know other people and some of them can be very useful. They have fingers in pies we know nothing about, so to have their ear can't do you any harm."

"I'll be guided by you then. Thanks, Ronny. I also owe you big time!"

*****

Mitch and I attacked the stern gland on the boat; a job we could do while waiting for any replies to our newspaper advertisement regarding the workshop.

It was a simple matter to prize out the old calking once we'd worked out how to remove the gasket cap, but then we had to move fast as the water gurgled through the bearings. We had already greased up the James Walker gasket rope, and after much cursing and swearing, we managed to refit the cap and adjust it so no water entered the boat, but that still left us with about two inches of water that needed to be pumped over the side."

"We need a battery and a twelve-volt bilge pump, Ed."

"We need shitloads more than just a pump and battery, we need to get her motor fired 'cos then she can generate her own bloody power. Get that sorted and we could do a bit of a refit, move her down to Ronny's, and Callum can come home."

"You miss him, don't you?"

"Yeah, I do. Much more than I thought. He phones every night and he's doing okay, but that's no substitute for...... whatever."

"Why don't we pull an extension cable over from the building and just buy a pump? Once the boat's dry you can work out what else needs to be done."

"What's that to do with Callum?"

"Loads. Just think about it for a moment. You want him back, well that's fucking obvious, but there's nowhere for him to doss that's safe. You and me get the boat dry, figure out what needs to be done to put her to rights and we get the boys to pitch in and help. You know they'd be up for it, and with you showing them what has to be done? Well, it makes for Callum's homecoming more realistic."

"Well I guess we could live without the engine for a bit; getting the interior fit to live in is the main thing right now."

*****

Three days later we had a dry boat so we dropped her into the water and spent what seemed like a lifetime looking for leaks. She remained dry, and so began the restoration of the boatman's cabin.

At the rear of this cabin was a stove that heated the interior, but also fed an oven and two hotplates for cooking food. This had never been used and the stone firebricks were in fine condition.

The interior woodwork was Ash and had stood the test of time pretty well, but all the varnishing and paintwork was either very faded or peeling away.

Muscle-power sorted that problem, and together with a stolen vacuum cleaner, we cleared up the mess.

Varnishing was easy – the paintwork not so easy but we managed to make it look reasonable. A piece of carpet offcut sorted the floor space and a lash-up of cables saw lighting and a couple of power points installed which signalled a green light for Callum to come home, but before I had the chance to call him, I had a text message from Pip.

"I need the use of your laptop. Call me after 8pm tonight and I'll explain why."

*****

"I hit the jackpot with our friend Carl. I've been working my nuts off what with getting the lawns looking good, cleaning up the fountain and getting that operational, not to mention weeding the driveway and raking the gravel; it does look the business rather than some sad old stately home. But that isn't what I needed to tell you. He noticed the effort I've been making, and instead of my pretend journey back home every night, he's offered me accommodation in the house. That means I have a set of keys and the code for the alarm."

"Nice work Pip. Have you had a chance to check the place out?"

"No, not yet. I've seen my room; it's like a palace, but other than being shown that and the kitchen, I've been too busy."

"You said you needed my laptop?"

"Yeah. I want to map the place, like an engineering drawing of the house, where the rooms are and a general layout of the interior. I might find something of interest that wouldn't otherwise be obvious."

"When do you need it and how do I get it to you?"

"Could we meet at your place in Solihull? Anytime works for me."

"I could be there for ten tomorrow morning?"

"Plan. I could buy my own with the dosh that Carl's shelling out, but your machine has the software I need."

"See you in the morning then, but please be careful, Pip? Just remember how vile that bloke is and what he's capable of."

"Always at the forefront of my thinking, maty. I like life too much to have it stolen from me."

*****

"So, it's going okay?"

"Hard work, but yeah it's starting to pay a dividend. I've asked if I might have a friend stay over sometimes; he wasn't overly enthusiastic, but relented when I told him he would pitch in and help straighten the house up."

"Couldn't be me. He knows who I am and where I'm from."

"I don't know? Get your hair cut in some sort of trendy style? Decent pair of jeans and shoes and he'll never recognise you from any other eighteen-year-old."

"Ha! You say."

"Act confident and look him in the eye like you're not bothered about talking to him. Works every time!"

"Yeah, well, it might at that. I miss Callum though? I wish he could come back?"

"Ahh. There's something you ought to know about Callum, Ed? He a fly-by-night, a free spirit. That's not to say he doesn't has a heart of gold, but he's suffered in his time and seeks comfort wherever he can find it. I'm sure he liked you well enough – even loved you, but he won't wait around too long before he's on the prowl again. He's in London now; the heart of the country where the possibilities for someone like him are never ending. It's another life down there, Ed, so you might have to come to terms with the fact that you've lost him."

"I thought that might happen the morning we saw him off on the train. It won't stop me from thinking about him; he saved me from myself that night and that's something I can never let go of."

"Lots of nice boys out there just waiting for you, Ed."

"Perhaps there is, but finding them might be a problem."

"Then let them find you."

*****

We had agreed that using my Christian name in front of Carl might not be the best move ever, so I assumed my middle name as a substitute. Daren Anderson sounded good to me, but it was essential that we didn't slip up.

Two days on, and with our cover story honed to perfection, we drove down the driveway to the house. Our story was that I had been taken in following the death of my mother – my father having disappeared from our lives some years earlier. This made life so much less complicated as it was partially true.

Like Pip, I was awaiting my exam results, and if I met with success, I wanted to train as a teacher. Again, this was sort of close as I had encouraged our boys into reading, writing and basic mathematics, but otherwise my background was that of your average kid.

Pip parked the Astra around the back of the house and took me through into the kitchen where Carl was sipping a mug of coffee.

"Morning Carl. This is my mate, Daren. He's more like my brother than a mate really. Daren, this is Carl who owns this pad."

We shook hands, then he looked me over. There wasn't even the slightest hint of recognition in his eyes, so satisfied I looked okay enough to be allowed in the building, he spoke.

"Nice to meet you, Daren. I hope you don't mind a bit of hard graft as this place needs some spit and polish before next weekend. Pip has worked a minor miracle with the gardens, but I'm expecting about a dozen people next Saturday, all of which will need clean and tidy rooms. Then there's the public rooms, dining hall and lounge, and if you do a good job of those, I might get you to open up the playroom and give that a spring clean.

Happy enough? Rate of pay is fifteen quid an hour. You book your own hours so don't go overboard with them. I reward honesty, so remember that and we'll get on famously."

"That's very generous. Thanks."

"Not especially, Daren? I expect you to have this joint looking the business by the time my guests arrive. That's a big ask, and a lot of work.

Pip? Can you handle driving an eighteen-seater minibus?"

"I've driven bigger stuff than that, so yeah, I can do that."

"Good. I have a driver who is going to get his marching orders later today so I'd like you to step into his shoes for Saturday morning and collect some people from Birmingham. You go with him, Daren. They're providing the cabaret or the entertainment for my guests, and I don't need any upsets. A fifty-quid bonus if you take them back in the morning, no questions asked, okay?"

*****

Shortly after, Carl climbed into a Range Rover Evoque and took off down the drive.

I breathed a sigh of relief.

"On the surface? A nice enough guy, but he's creepy, Pip......
very fucking creepy!"

"Can't argue with that, but he's paying us loads of dosh, he trusts us which gives us the opportunity to go snooping around, so not all bad?"

"Get the graft out of the way, then go looking around.

What's your take on this cabaret thing?"

"I hope to fuck I'm totally wrong, but I think the Cabaret are young boys who will be providing the entertainment, and what makes things even worse? We're collecting them like lambs to the slaughter."

"Don't use that word Pip. I'm having enough difficulty keeping my breakfast down without you talking of slaughter."

"Relax. Nothing like that's going to happen. Callum reckoned that Carl hosted very private sessions if that was the agenda. We do our job, make notes, do a head-count there and back, and maybe report our findings, but at all times we play it cool like we're totally unaware of what's going down."

Chapter Eighteen.

On my list of jobs to be done were all the guest rooms, dining room and library to be vacuumed and dusted. I had also been asked to do much the same to the Play Room and bar, and when the dray arrived, to supervise the off-loading of barrels of beer and bottles of wine and spirits into the cellar.

The guest rooms; all eighteen of them took me a complete day and the best part of the evening to get them to an acceptable standard, the reception rooms took less time, and by the time the dray arrived, I'd finished them.

"I'll take a break from gardening, Ed. I've never been inside that room as I thought the alarm code might be different. Obviously, it's not, so I'll take some photos."

"What if he's got CCTV running?"

"We'll have time enough to check for cameras, but then why would he want to monitor that room and not the others?"

"Can't answer that. He's given us the freedom of the entire house except for his private suite, and none of that is on a separate system."

The delivery was easy, so while I stacked the barrels and racked the wines, Pip, camera in hand, went to explore the Play Room.

"Very plush, but nothing I didn't expect to find. Well, that isn't entirely truthful, I did find something. The whole place is wired to video monitors, there are cameras all over the place, sophisticated and very expensive fuckers as well! I think he monitors everything, keeps it on a hard drive and either sells it back to the punters, or uses it to blackmail them, but it isn't like CCTV.

Oh, to have the alarm code to his office!"

"Or a video camera of our own."

"Yeah, that as well, but it's too late to think about that now. This gig kicks off tomorrow and the place will be swarming with security if our guess is correct about what's likely going on here."

*****

We met in the kitchen at six the following morning and already some of Carl's men had arrived. One acknowledged Pip but then asked who I was. He looked on a clip folder and nodded his head.

ip joined me moments later.

"He was just checking you out, but now we'd better get going and collect the cabaret. They're not Brummies' as we suspected, we've got to go to Stafford then back down to Wolverhampton to collect them. I'm happy about that, I didn't need to see anyone I knew."

"Knew?"

"Yeah, knew or know. Lots of the lads sell themselves. They start aged twelve when their goods are saleable, then knock it on the head once they start to mature. Nothing unusual there, Ed."

"Did you ever......?"

"No, not my thing. I mean, look at me? Do I look like the type dirty old perverts are after? No, I play the game, the one where I can talk myself into situations, and hopefully, talk myself out of them. I survive using my brain, not my body! Less of a risk, and definitely more lucrative."

"You're Okay-looking?"

"Ha! Compare me to the kids we're going to collect, then comment. Callum was stunning when he was thirteen, but still marketable now aged seventeen. South-east Asian. No body hair, nice and slim, nice complexion and a big dick. He's the exception that proves the rule. I'm straight as an arrow, but some of these young boys we'll see today? Well, even I could find myself questioning my sexuality!"

"Never!"

"Who was that Greek bloke who said, 'Women are for duty but boys are for pleasure?' Sometimes I think their logic was sound as a pound and it's us who are all fucked up about stuff. Who knows, but although though I'm not gay, even if I can appreciate a great looking kid."

"Still, it's totally wrong to traffic these kids just so some wealthy weirdo can get his jollies."

"Agreed, but some of them actually enjoy it. From what little Callum told me about it, there's very little coercion and the boys are generally treated very well by their abusers; one reason they come back for more I guess. Some of the men involved don't want to touch the boys. They prefer to see a little boy-on-boy action...... probably can't get it up, truth be told!"

"But all those video cameras. He could be making more by selling the footage than he is by hosting these parties!"

"Yeah, well, helicopters and top of the range Mercedes off-roaders don't come cheap, Ed. Then you have the minibus and the four Range Rover Evoques garaged here, and what must this pad cost to maintain? The rateable value alone must cost bucket loads, then there's heating and lighting and general upkeep? You should do some digging into his business interests and see what pops up. Carl Stephen Matterson. Google him later, huh?"

*****

We did the collection run; most of the boys seemed animated and not at all fazed by what the day / night had in store for them. Some were obviously older than they looked, probably fourteen or fifteen, but clever use of foundation cream and shaved of body hair, under lighting they'd look good enough. By contrast, some were really young, like eleven or twelve, but one lad stood out from the crowd as he definitely wasn't very happy.

I tried talking to him, but he clammed up on me.

"You can talk to me, you know? We're just the drivers, and nothing to do with what goes on later?"

"Just leave me be, alright? I'll be okay once we get there!"

"Please yourself. I was only trying to help. I'm here if you wanna chat things over, okay?"

As I squeezed past the rows of seats, one of the older boys collared me.

"I overheard that conversation."

"Yeah, so now you'll go telling Carl!"

"What? You have to be joking, right? We do what we do, take the money and run. None of us like this Carl guy, he's creepy and dangerous if you ask me. Wee Donny is one of the punters favourites, and when I tell you this guy is hung like a horse, I mean, he's fucking huge, but he pounds Donny's arse without a care in the world."

"So, why does he keep coming?"

"Simple. His Dad gets paid a fortune for sending him. Donny's gay, but all he wants is someone to love him, not destroy his ass."

"Oh fuck. I wish I could get him away to somewhere safe."

"You know somewhere like that?"

"Yeah. We've kinda fostered kids, like street kids. Our place is safe as houses."

"Want me to talk with Donny? He talks about running away from home, but he's young and doesn't understand how the world works."

"Would he trust us enough? He probably thinks we're in league with this Carl bloke, and that might scare him off."

"But you're not, are you? One thing I've learned is how to read people, and you don't come across as being a part of this."

"Between you and me, we'd love to sink him. He's got a snuff out on a friend of ours, and for my money, Carl's bollocks nailed to the nearest tree would just be for openers."

"Let me talk to Donny then. I'll see what he thinks."

*****

I think that Donny was so shit-scared, he'd go with any plan to get him away from the party.

We agreed to drop him off at my place in Solihull where he would be met by Buba and Ian, two of the toughest guys I know. Buba was massive, and being black, he was a formidable man. Ian was a bruiser of epic proportions and I'd had serious reservations about allowing him into our group, but the old adage, Never judge a book by its cover rings true because he was really okay, and would be the ideal person to look after Donny.

Carl wasn't pleased that one of his 'Cabaret' was a no-show, in fact he was furious.

"Jesus Christ! I could do without one of them, maybe two, but that kid not turning up is going to cost me a packet!"

"Sorry, Carl, but not knowing where he lived, we just waited around until the last minute before we had to get back or risk being late."

"Not your fault, Darren. You did what I asked you to do.

What are you planning to do tonight? This gig is an all-nighter, so if you want to go home, then fine, but just get back here for midday so you and Pip can do the return run. The other option is that you stay here, but if you did, you'd have to keep to your rooms."

"We'll head back home I think. Pip's anxious to see his girlfriend and I'm bushed and could use some sleep.

Yeah. Midday sounds like a plan."

*****

We decided that rather than going back to Digbeth, we'd camp out at Solihull. The car would be hidden away in the garage, and besides, it was nearer when it came to going back the next morning. Buba announced his intention of taking the train back to town as he had work in the morning, but Ian volunteered to stay with us then hang around until we got back from doing the return trip.

Donny looked a tad more comfortable than he did on the bus, so I thought it was time I put some questions to him.

"You okay? The guys been looking after you alright?"

"Yeah, they've been cool. I'm just worried about my old chap and what he might do when I'm a no-show tomorrow afternoon."

224

"Well, I was coming to that, Donny. The way I see it, he can hardly report you as a run-away to the police, there's too much risk involved. We picked you up from Stafford and you're as far away from there as we can get you. I mean, he's not likely to go scouring the suburbs of Birmingham, is he? If he came looking for you, he'd look closer to home turf where you knew the area."

"So, I stay here?"

"No. This is like halfway house. Once Pip and I get back to-morrow we'll take you to our place in Brum. You'll be amongst kids your own age who know all the angles. You'll be safe there."

"Thanks. I owe you."

"You owe us sweet fuck-all. Just hunker down and stick to the few rules we have and everything will be peachy."

"What rules do you have?"

"No so many. The main thing is not to go doing anything that might bring us to the attention of the authorities. We don't need the law sniffing around. The other boys know their way around, so follow their lead and if you have any concerns talk either to me or Pip. We'll have to find something to occupy your time or you'll go stir-crazy, but it's all for the good of the group; nothing that's going to stress you."

"You're nice, and I'm sorry for being an arsehole on the bus. I'm not used to being around nice people."

"Forget it like it never happened. You're nice too. Very nice in fact."

Ian came in from the garden and parked himself at the kitchen table.

"Anyone fancy a Chinese carry-out? I'm bloody staving."

"Sounds good to me. There's a menu on the pin board."

Donny reached for his wallet. "Let me pay. It's the least I can do."

"Not tonight, sunshine. If you wanna dib in another time then fine, but your first night is on me."

"Second night actually. Buba cooked for us last night; he's one awesome chef I reckon!"

"He is that. Just wait until you try his stock pot. Your taste buds will love you forever!"

*****

By ten-thirty we were ready to hit the sack. Ian opted to sleep in the lounge just in case we had unwelcome visitors during the night, Pip took the front bedroom, and as we'd chucked out the three beds in the remaining spare rooms, that left Donny having to share with me.

Pip chuckled as he made his way upstairs. "Nighty-night. Don't make too much noise, will you!"

Donny looked first at Pip, then me. "What's he talking about?"

"Ah well! In case you hadn't guessed, I'm gay, and he thinks I'm going to jump you!"

"Cool. Not on our first date though!"

"You're funny. I really do like you, but we'd better turn in. Another busy day ahead."

*****

The night was sticky and humid and I would've much preferred sleeping in the buff, but out of modesty, both Donny and I had kept our underpants on.

I woke to find him spooned into my back, and it felt good and I wondered what Callum's reaction might be if he saw us like this but then dismissed it from my mind. He'd left me for pastures new and doubtless he would've found someone else by now.

I'd missed cuddling up to him, but maybe, just maybe I'd found someone new myself.

I looked at my watch. Seven-thirty and I needed the bathroom, so I disentangled myself, took a shower and got dressed leaving Donny to sleep on. Both Pip and Ian were already up and about. Ian offered me a mug of tea while Pip took the rubbish out to the bins.

"Donny's getting all worked up about what his old man will do when he doesn't show his face at home later. Any bright ideas, Ian?"

"Best you talk to Pip, Ed. He's the bright ideas guy, but personally, I'd be more bothered about what this Carl character might do once he realises he's been had. He's going to be giving Donny's old man a grilling, and once he finds out that Donny was taken to the meeting point but presumably did a runner, he'll go mental."

"Might backfire on us as well."

"Why? It's hardly your fault that he didn't show up, but he might set his goons out searching for him. Loose cannons are very dangerous, and in his case, if Donny goes off half-cocked and blabs to the Old Bill, he's looking at a life sentence. Whichever way you look at it, Ed, Donny is going to be like the fox running from the hounds unless you and Pip manage to spike this Carl's guns first."

*****

"Plan A. We get Donny to write a letter to his old chap which we post once we get to Stafford. Two reasons for doing this, the first being that Donny threatens to go to the police if *anyone* goes looking for him, the second reason is that because the letter will have been franked in Stafford, everyone will assume that's where he's hiding out."

"So, what's Plan B, Pip?"

"There isn't one, so if A doesn't work, we're deep in shit and then some."

"Wouldn't it be good if we could go straight to the police. I've got this horrible feeling that we won't find anything at the house. Who in their right minds would allow two lads to have access if there was something incriminating lurking in a cupboard somewhere? If there is something, it'll be in his private apartments and we don't know the alarm code, but if that was me, I'd not even keep anything there, I'd have it stored away in a safe deposit box."

"You're probably right, but going to the police with little or next to sod-all evidence barring the word of a thirteen-year-old boy and our suspicions would be madness."

"What about the other boys? They might know something we don't? They can't all be under orders from pervy fathers, so how are they recruited; where does Carl find them?"

"Dangerous tactic. The fewer people in the loop, the more we're not implicated. I wouldn't go talking to them if I were you…… but if one of them volunteered information? Those two who wanted us to hide Donny. They might be of help?"

"I'll beg the question on the way back. Also, I've thought of a way where we could find an honest copper. I'm still formulating plans, but I'll tell you all about it once I'm happy we won't get annihilated."

*****

"Where's Donny?"

"Let's just say he's out of harm's way, happy and well looked after, shall we?"

"You two are for real, right? We wouldn't want to see him harmed."

"We're doing our best, but here's where it becomes tricky. We need help if we're going to bust Carls arse. Suspicions and hearsay evidence just won't cut it. He'll have heavy guns to look out for him, solicitors and barristers to destroy our story. We need fact, hard evidence if we're to down the bastard."

"So, you expect us to divvy in?"

"I expect absolutely nothing. I realise enough to know you make good money from what he has you do. I go trashing his operation and your toast, but I want you to think about the likes of Donny who doesn't want to be involved. I need names, how you were recruited and by whom, who attends those parties, addresses and email – anything solid that might help."

"MacDonald's. Birmingham Road Wolverhampton on the A41 at four tomorrow afternoon. Meet us there but don't be late."

*****

We dropped the boys where we'd found them then took the bus back to the house. The place was silent, locked up and deserted, so we garaged the bus and took the Astra back to Solihull to collect Donny and Ian.

No news and no visitors, so we grabbed a swift coffee, tidied up and left for Digbeth.

"You're being very kind to me, all of you are. I'm still scared my old man will find me though?"

"We have contingency plans to head him off, Donny. The first was your letter, which if nothing else should buy us time. There's other stuff, but that can wait.

Where do you go to school?"

"Don't you mean Used to go? Park Avenue Comprehensive until my old man decided home education was better."

"He taught you?"

"Yeah. He was a science teacher until he got caught tinkering around with little boys. He went to court, but someone stumped up enough cash for him to get the services of a swanky brief. They got him off on a technicality but he could never teach again."

"Any idea who this *someone* was?"

"Nah. By that time his hands were all over me and the next thing I knew I was farmed out to those creeps."

"By way of payback?"

"I reckon so. They had money and I was cute."

"You're still cute, at least I think you are."

Donny blushed ten shades of red. "You're not all bad yourself, so stop embarrassing me!"

"Sorry. Do you think your dear father knows who's paying him all this money?"

"He has to know. He looks to his bank account after every party to see if there's money enough to pay the bills, buy drugs and get smashed on. He knows alright!"

"So, we do a little bit of housebreaking, find his statements and we're in business."

"He banks electronically. I know the details if you have a PC and an internet connection."

"Got both. We'll take a gander once we're back."

*****

Most of the journey lacked conversation, but then my phone squawked at me.

It was Callum calling me.

"Hey! How's things in the scary city then?"

"Much like Brum except bigger. Look, I want to apologise to you. I'm a fucking disaster when it comes to keeping in touch, it's just that this place offers up so many chances, I lose track of time."

"You're forgiven, but why now are you calling, nice though it is?"

"Information. I heard on the grapevine you and Pip are out to nail that asshole Carl. I can help you with hard evidence, names, addresses, contact details and more, but the downside is this. I won't come back to Birmingham, not ever. I'm in enough shit what with the snuff going down, and if I make it so as you can get a case together, my arse won't be worth the pants I'm wearing."

"I understand you perfectly, but how did you find out what we were up to?"

"The lads on the bus. I know both of them, we've done parties together in the past. They called me to find out if you were on the level. I gave you a glowing reference by the way! Trust them, Ed, but they're sorta shitting themselves right now just in case someone susses out what's going on."

"Thanks, Callum. Always my saviour! How do I contact you?"

"I'll call you. Safer that way. We can meet some place off the beaten track where I can give you everything you need, but then I'll have to cut and run. I won't see you again and that hurts me, but look on the bright side? You have Donny now and he's a gorgeous lad, so take care of him.

Gotta go now. Laterz, Ed, I still love you."

*****

The first task as soon as we arrived home was to get Donny settled in. Most of the boys were out with a handful of them cleaning up the engine that powered the workshop so I made the introductions then took him to the kitchen for a mug of coffee and a chat.

"Did you ever meet Callum?"

"No, but I've heard about him, everyone on the circuit had. He was a legend almost."

"Well, this was the place where he used to doss. He took me in when I first ran away from home, looked after me and showed me the ropes. I had the feeling I wasn't exactly welcome, but he persevered with me and became very close."

"S,o where is he now? The rumour floating around is he went up north."

"I can't tell you where he is, it's too dangerous. If certain people got hold of the truth, his life wouldn't be worth crap. He's my friend and I don't want to see him hurt."

"Carl?"

"I'll tell you what happened.

I ran away because my Mum had taken up with a bloke. I wouldn't have minded had he been reasonable, but he was a drug addict and an alcoholic and he dragged my Mum down to the same pathetic level. He used to threaten me with a knife, steal my wallet and trash my room. He smashed up all my furniture, wrecked my laptop and ripped up my clothes, then one day I'd had enough. I grabbed what little cash I had hidden away and ran. No game plan, no idea of how I was going to survive, but anything had to be preferable to staying at home.

I found myself here and Callum took me in.

I knew my Mum was in hospital. She'd OD'd on drugs, but when I found out she'd been sectioned, I called the hospital to find out how she was doing. Well, she wasn't going to be allowed out, even if she made it through detox. She would most likely end up in an institution, but during one of her lucid moments, she wrote me a note which the hospital sent to my old house address. Pip and I went and picked it up and what went down following that isn't important, except we found lover boys mobile phone and a very cryptic voicemail with threats to his life if he didn't cough up some money he owed.

Thing is, Callum listened to that message and recognised the voice. It was our friend Carl. Callum kept this to himself for ages, only telling Pip and me after we'd visited the house where the parties are held. He already knew he'd been selected for a snuffing which is why he went into hiding, but now we were looking at what can only be described as a massive drug organisation plus a child sex ring. Carl's operation had to enormous, and the possibility of Callum being seen in Birmingham was very real, so it was decided that he should disappear until we could get enough together to hopefully nail Carls arse to the floor.

Perhaps now you can understand that I can't tell you where he's gone. We don't know just how far reaching Carls contacts are or what else he might be involved in, Donny."

"That all rings true. The men paid a fortune to attend those parties, but everything was on tap. There was the sex, but also there was enough booze sloshing around to pickle most of the West Midlands. Then there were drugs, anything they wanted was supplied. You could've cut the air with a knife there was so much dope being smoked. There were guys shooting up, snorting lines of cocaine, you name it, it was probably going on, and all included in the price."

"You mentioned bank accounts. If I hook up my laptop, would you mind accessing your fathers account?"

"Sure. His account number is 00843854, sort code 69-45-01 and the access number isn't a number it's my initials followed by my date of birth, so DAMB13062003."

"So that's Donald what?"

"Donald Adrian MacBride, and in case your maths is poor, I'm thirteen nudging fourteen."

"I did work that out, but thanks anyway!

*****

Let's see what we have here. Bank of Scotland, Inverness branch. Account balance is a little over ten grand with the last deposit paid on April 30th by...... Who on earth is or are Greycoats?"

"How much was paid in?"

"Two and a half grand."

"That's them then."

"That's some paycheque for twenty-four hour's work!"

"The bastard who took a shine to me is rich. He turns up in a Roller and each visit it's a different one."

"Okay. We have a name of an organisation, so let's see if there's anything on the internet about them."

We searched the web, but aside from two schools, the names of which came close like The Bluecoat School, an up market private school for boys and Greycoats School in Hampshire, both with exceptional pedigrees, there was nothing.

Next to the Companies House website. Here we had a degree of success. A limited liability company operating out of Coventry that listed itself as an Entertainment Organiser came up on the screen. We dug further only to discover that the three Directors were a Carl Stephens and a Sir Alfred Morrison-Penrose together with Donny's father.

Well, that pegged our Carl firmly to the mast, even though the name had been massaged, but who was this Sir Alfred bloke? I did a search for his name, and BINGO!

Rear Admiral Sir Alfred Morrison-Penrose Rtrd. Born July 1944. Joined the Royal Navy as an officer cadet aged fourteen gaining rapid promotion to Lieutenant Commander (Baltic Fleet), Commander (Southern Oceans), Captain (Mediterranean) then Rear Admiral (Whitehall) then subsequently put out to grass on full pension. Read into that what you will, but our guess was that he transgressed, maybe something too hot to handle then found himself side-lined.

There were also a couple of photos of him which Donny looked at.

"Airbrushed, but that's him."

"So, what have we got here. A non-trading company shoves a significant amount of money into your dad's account. All the directors are directly connected with these parties? Might it be that all the other boys are paid in the same way? Carl is a director of all of them with different second directors of different companies that all pay taxes so keeping them off the HMRC's radar, the second or third director takes a legitimate tax-free bonus and job's a good'un! No tax liability, no mess and no suspicions."

"The only way to prove your theory is to ask the boys when you meet them at Mackies...... see if they know names and do the same search."

"Problem with that is we won't have any bank details to show us what company is shelling out.

I'll think on that one for now."

Chapter Nineteen

I waltzed around the knotty question of where Donny would spend his first night with us. The boys he had managed to meet were sympathetic and accepted his presence without a backward glance, but that said, he was still away from everything he knew, he was with strangers and nervous regarding his father's reaction. Pip was all for going to Stafford to stake out his home address, but had a rethink when it was gently pointed out that there was a distinct possibility that Carl might also be paying his Dad a visit and recognise the car.

I offered Donny the option of sleeping in the communal area or bed down beside me as I had erected a studding wall to give me some privacy, - he elected to be with me.

I wondered why I was pleased about this. Callum and I did it every night, but I never got excited over the prospect of sharing beds with him. I loved Callum, I really did, but sex with him was something I studiously avoided. Now I found myself getting very aroused, my heart felt funny and I never wanted bedtime to come so soon, but I had work to do. I had to read to the boys, even if they were more than capable of reading by themselves by now.

At ten-thirty, Mitch went through and powered down the generator while Pip banked up the fire. Gradually the place fell silent, so Donny and I slipped out and got changed ready for bed. Lack of central heating made us hurry along, but then I asked him if there was anything he'd left at home he might like us to rescue.

"I don't have that much. Some clothes might be nice, especially if we get colder weather. I wouldn't mind having my laptop, but I reckon my Dad will be going crazy and looking through my emails trying to find out where I might've gone. He'll probably junk it once he sees there's nothing to find."

"We can sort clothing for you and you can use my laptop until we can find a replacement for yours. How about things like your bank account, cheque books or deposit books?"

"Do all that electronically. I change the access code after every deposit so Dad wouldn't be able to pilfer anything."

"You ought to check your balance in the morning just in case he's smarter than you think."

We climbed into bed and turned off the torch leaving a nightlight glimmering in the alcove.

"Could you kiss me, Ed?"

I leaned over and sought out his lips. I'd kissed Callum in the past, but nothing could compare with this. Callum's kisses were urgent and really eager, but Donny was warm and gentle and I had to break off after a few minutes.

"Oh, God, Donny? That was too much for me! I'm not used to this stuff, and you'll have to take it easy or I'll get carried away."

"I'll wait for you. I've never felt this way before about anyone. Blokes at the parties didn't wait, and if they hadn't already cum in their pants, they were all over me like a rash. I suppose it's all I've ever known so I do what they did to me."

"Well, I'm not the party animal so things are going to be different. I feel odd when I look at you, I want to say I love you but

I've only known you for three days and I don't think that's how love works. I don't want to go full steam ahead only to find it doesn't work between us."

"No one has ever cared about me before, so I guess this is like a game-changer. I used to get ill before a party. Not ill like running a temperature, but ill like throwing up at the prospect of what was going to happen. I don't feel that way about you, and actually, I want you to take me.

But I can wait, Ed."

"I'm afraid you're going to have to. I would have to be absolutely sure it's what you want. I can't risk hurting you, or for that matter, hurting myself. I have feelings too, remember?"

*****

I woke laying on my back with Donny on his side and his arm draped over my stomach. His breathing was deep and even so I guessed he wasn't ready to wake for a while yet. I needed coffee, so I slipped quietly out of bed, got dressed and made my way outside.

Pip had beaten me to the post. He pointed to the coffee pot, so I helped myself to a brew.

"The real deal there, Ed, not your instant rubbish."

"Where did it come from?"

"Buba persuaded Ronny to go up-market and offer this as an alternative. He started his shift at six this morning then dropped this off at seven to see what we thought of it."

"It's good. Get a real caffeine hit of this stuff!"

"You're not the hyperactive type."

"Not as a rule, but shove a few spoonful's of sugar in it and I'd be bouncing off the walls."

"How's Donny holding up?"

"Still asleep, but he seemed fine last night."

"It's just that by now, the shit will have definitely hit the proverbial fan and that might make him even more skittish than he was yesterday."

"Very possibly, but what choices did we have? Personally, I don't care if his Dad gets a bloody good pasting off Carl, no one has the right to farm their own children out for sex, but what does concern me is this. If he does a good enough job in convincing Carl that Donny's disappearing act had nothing to do with him, Carl's not the type to just let it ride and there's always the possibility that he'll get his guys to come after him."

"Why would he want to do that? Donny's just a kid and kids go missing all the time, so why waste resources?"

"Something Ian said about loose cannons being dangerous."

"So Donny has a name, but then so did Callum, and Carl never went after him?"

"No, but Callum was running scared. Carl knew him well enough to know that his distrust of the police played right into his hands and Callum wouldn't go near a police station, he'd lay low and wait until the dust settled. Donny's different. He has no reason not to trust the police. Up until last night, he'd lived at home with his father, getting a good education and had an unblemished record. No, Ian's right. Donny represents a real danger to Carl."

"They would still have a job making a connection between us and his disappearance or even where we are."

"Unless we've been unbelievably careless. Is the Astra still registered in Solihull?"

"Yep. Cost too much to insure if I used this address. This is an unsavoury area in case you hadn't noticed."

"That guy from the museum. What if he'd been at the party and recognised me?"

"When? No one had arrived when we dropped the boys off and there wasn't anyone at the house barring Carl and his band of merry men when we collected them for the return journey. I think you're spooking yourself unnecessarily."

"How I hope you're right, Pip."

*****

As it happened, we didn't get any unexpected visitors, so mid-afternoon Pip and I left to meet the boys from Wolverhampton. We arrived on time and the lads were waiting for us.

"How's Donny shaping up?"

"He's fine. He got a good night's rest, and when we left him, he was helping one or our boys mixing concrete to repair the wharf. He's okay and with people who will look out for him."

"That's good to know 'cos all of us were rounded up this morning and given the Third-Degree. Carl's seriously got his panties in a knot over this!"

"No one grassed us up though?"

"Believe it. If anyone had said anything we'd all be toast by now. If one kid opened his gob then suspicion would be on all of us, and as you might have gathered, Carl's an animal and he'd take us out without batting so much as an eyelid."

"So, are you happy enough to help us out with names?"

"On one condition. If thing start to heat up, we'll need a safe-house."

"If any of you have worries about your safety then call me on the number on this card. We have room enough to put you up plus the only access is off the canal or through high steel gates topped with razor wire."

"Game on then. We've written down what names we know and we've got a couple of addresses. There are others who go there but some we don't know or only go there to watch the action so we can't help you with those.

Just be warned, some of these blokes are heavyweight solicit-ors, barristers, clergy, senior members of the armed forces and some politicians. Get your strategy wrong and you're fucked, they'll eat you for breakfast."

"We hear you. We realised there might be heavy guns in-volved. I guess you must have a tidy bank balance to attend one of those gigs, but there's one other thing I'd be interested to un-derstand, and that's how you were recruited."

"Word of mouth mostly. A kid at school, maybe someone like Donny, is paid to go around all the boys in his school who like a bit of cock, make them an offer they can't refuse, and the rest is history. Some lads get picked up in public toilets selling them-selves, others are forced into it by parents or uncles and some just plain enjoy it and look on the dark web for anything that might be going down."

"Not helpful. We were hoping to discover a direct link that might take us back to Carl."

"He's too clever for that. He's not going to involve himself at ground level."

"Nobody is able to cover all bases. There has to be a chink in his armour somewhere."

"Just watch your back. He's a fucking Psychopath, and a very dangerous psychopath to boot.

Might be an idea if you fucked off now. If we hear of anything interesting, we'll shout you."

*****

"At least we have names if little else. This is going to take time to figure out."

"Might I make a suggestion, Ed?"

"Fire away. I need help here."

"First off, I'm not that computer-literate. I know the basics but you need someone better than me to bounce ideas off. I'll always be around if you need me, no worries there, but why not involve Donny? He's as bright as ninepence, knows computers, so it stands to reason that as he has a vested interest in sinking Carl, for my dosh, he's your man."

"That, my man, is a very good idea and I feel ashamed I didn't think of it first!"

"Pip the genius strikes again...... until it comes to computers and what it takes to rid myself of acne!"

"Love ya anyway...... despite your zits!"

*****

"Are you up for helping me then?"

"Deffo. When do we start?"

"Not tonight. We've got to get dinner, and then there's reading to the lads. Tomorrow morning, *IF* you manage to wake before late afternoon will do!"

"Hey! I wasn't that late up? It was around...... yeah. Okay I was tardy. I got up at just gone eleven. I promise to be earlier to-morrow."

"Donny? It doesn't matter! You're free to do your own thing here. Just pitch in with the housework and everything's cool! Yesterday was really stressful for everyone, and you needed to get your rest. Tomorrow you'll feel much fresher and better able to apply yourself but we have to trade ideas here and you can't do that if you're feeling too knackered to concentrate on the job in hand."

"Got it. I'll go and help Buba get dinner on the go."

"He'll appreciate that."

I read to the boys but to be truthful, my mind was on other things and I was pleased when I'd finished the book and people disappeared to take showers and head to bed.

If Donny was tired, then I needed a brain transplant. Tiredness overtook me and I just propped myself against the fireplace and zoned out.

An hour later, and as I hadn't come to bed, Donny gave me a shake.

"I need my sleep? Come on, Ed. Do yourself a favour and come to bed."

That was me until nine the following morning. Donny was already up and about which made me feel guilty about crashing out last evening.

Pip looked at me then took his phone from his pocket.

"Doc? Pip here…… yeah, Pip as in…… Pip? Have you been drinking?

I need you to come over if you're fit enough. One of our number is about to collapse on us. Get a grip? This is Edward we're talking about here. He doesn't do drugs, never touches the bottle but I'm very concerned about him. Yes, we'll pay you. Just get you pervy arse over here and fast!"

No good. I was about to pass out, but I remained conscious enough to respond.

"I'll be fine after some coffee. The dodgy doctor I don't need."

Then my world went black.

*****

"Well, dear boy. What a fine state to get yourself in I must say."

I made to sit up, but DD pushed me back onto the pillows.

"What's going on? Where the hell am I?"

"In reverse order, you are at my country cottage in Worcestershire, and you are not a well boy. You are suffering from blood poisoning brought about from what I can only assume is direct contact with a substance we call PHDS. PHDS is used as a deep cleanser, the sort of stuff used to disinfect the hospitals in Africa during the Ebola epidemic. Kills ninety-nine percent of all household germs don't you know!

My wit is undoubtedly lost on you, but the sad fact is, it's more than capable of killing your immunity responses as well as germs and if dear Phillip here hadn't come to your aid? No nice bed for you, a cold slab in a mortuary would be your resting place now. I'm going to give you an injection of a mild sedative. This will allow your system to recover sufficiently enough to get you on your feet, maybe twenty-four hours at most.

Now it's time to say night-night to Phillip and your delectable young boyfriend, who I will not sully. He's suffered enough, and he loves you.

Sleep well dear boy."

*****

"How are you feeling Edward? You've been asleep for over thirty-six hours."

"Groggy. My head feels like I'm living in a fog, Doc."

"Hardly surprising, my friend. The toxicity of PHDS together with Diamorphine is a powerful combination and you will feel off-colour for a few days yet I'm afraid. On a more positive note, you don't appear to have suffered any complications that might require hospitalisation, so I expect you to be running around like spring chicken in a day or so. I'm keeping you on a saline drip, but otherwise I'm taking you off all other medication."

"Spring chicken? I'm not at all sure I like that analogy!"

"Profuse apologies. No offence intended."

"This PDHS. How did I contaminate myself?"

"In truth, I cannot be 100% sure, but that cut on your ankle looks recent. Do you know how and where you came by that injury?"

248

"Yes. It happened on Sunday morning. I tripped up some steps."

"I don't need to know where, but was it the sort of place that appeared to be in need of such a toxic cleaning agent?"

"It was just a house, a very big house, and I can't think why...... wait a minute? There might've been part of it that needed a going-over?"

"Again, I don't need details, but PDHS is a controlled chemical. You have to be licenced to buy it, and if the purpose didn't match the stringent criteria as laid down by the government, it would've been very difficult to obtain."

"Black market?"

"If you have the necessary funds, dear boy, you can get hold of just about anything."

"Thanks Doc. You might've just hit upon a missing piece in a complicated jigsaw."

"Pleased I could be of assistance."

"There is just one other thing? If you wanted to erase DNA evidence from a crime scene, could using that chemical have the desired effect?"

"Oh, absolutely, but DNA hides away in the smallest of places. A microscopic fibre can yield up just as much data as a cart load of the stuff. If you think that simply washing somewhere down is sufficient, then think again. The only reason criminals escape justice is because Crime Scene Officers and scientists are slap-dash. Sufficient evidence can be found between floorboards, behind skirting boards, inside wall sockets and light fittings, just about any small crevice will hide something of interest."

"You're a star! Thanks, Doc!"

"No thanks required. I'm just a man that loves young boys and made a catastrophic error of judgement. I can't deny what I am, nothing I can do to stop my attraction towards them, but I was stupid and I paid the price by serving eighteen months at Her Majesty's pleasure then stuck off by the Medical Council. I'm not a bad man, my DNA dictates who I'm attracted to, Edward, so it's out of my hands."

"I hear you. I'm going to rethink things following that."

*****

Doc sent me home once my recovery was well on track. I think I'd misjudged him and tried to apologise, but he was contrite and told me that he was still paying the price for stepping beyond the acceptable. No one had been hurt, the boy in question was a willing participant, in fact their relationship had been on-going for a number of months with the boy visiting his surgery out of hours and at his own volition. His mistake was leaving a light on and the blinds not fully closed.

Enough said.

Donny had been hard at work collating what little information we had so we set about the job of making up a spread sheet that detailed names, addresses if we had them, email addresses if we had them, then with blank columns we could fill in with possible links to companies, cross referencing them to anything we could unearth about Carl. Other connections such as solicitors, accountants, anything that might flag up constants.

Donny was mustard with computers. In truth, he was way better than I was and I thought I was pretty good, so we went for broke and bought another system so we could work separately and merge files once we had something that looked promising.

Names supplied by the Wolverhampton lads revealed occupations, and in some cases, business interests with all of them holding down positions of authority and influence. Some could be linked to Carl and the myriad of companies that he was on the board of directors of, but these guys were shown as customers rather than associates so we assumed that these were the ones paying for services rendered rather than being the providers.

We were running out of ideas. We were running out of inspiration, that was until one night, sleeping peacefully in our bed, Donny woke with a start and ran from the room.

I woke and followed him moments later. Donny was hunched over his machine, bottom lip between his teeth as he waited for something to download.

He glanced up as I walked through.

"Approaching this from the wrong angle. We should look at this as a pyramid and begin at the top, not at the base. The base is so cluttered up with names, companies and irrelevant detail, it's diverted our attention from the one person who matters. Now, if we start at the top, Carl has so many business interests, fingers in so many pies it's frightening. Take the house as a prime example. He doesn't own it outright, he's just one of a number of people who are trustees of a charity that claim they're going to use it as a school for under privileged children. Second is his biggest business interest which is registered as an off-shore jobbie. The problem with this is, it's registered in Equatorial New Guinea which is one of the few countries that refused to sign up to the open banking agreement.

"So, we're headed down a blind alley?"

Not necessarily. We have the registration numbers of what vehicles he uses. I'm going to try to hack in to the DVLA database and find out who they're registered to and to what addresses."

"Isn't that risky?"

"Not if I'm careful. With luck they won't know anything about it. Do you want to go back to bed or are you going to stay up?"

"Wide awake now so I might just as well get dressed and follow up on some of these businesses we haven't looked at yet."

*****

By the end of a long and very tiring day we had mapped out what looked like a family tree with Carl at the top, what business interests we could identify, his co-directors together with some sort of customer base which we assumed were boy's parents, relatives or whoever was pimping them out, but other than building up a better picture of Carl's complex operation, we still didn't have very much to go on.

From what we could understand, all these blind companies that sported names like such-and-such holdings, or so-and-so trading, all submitted regular tax returns and accounts which was a cute move as it wouldn't alert Her Majesty's Revenue and Customs to any suspicious activities, just small businesses keeping to the rules.

Donny managed to hack in to the DVLA database and discovered that all the vehicles were registered to another company, the address of which was Berkhamstead in Hertforshire. Avant Executive Vehicles Limited appeared to be a legitimate business with a long trading history that also submitted regular tax returns and accounts. It came as no surprise to see that Carl was listed as the Managing Director although the Company Secretary together with the names of the other Directors were new to us.

We Googled them but came up with squat.

"This is ridiculous. It's as if he's built a maze full of stuff to deliberately muddy the waters. We've not managed to find anything other than what appear to be a string of legitimate businesses, names that reveal nothing when we Google them, upmarket cars that we can safely assume are leased, in fact the only dodgy enterprise is this charity for underprivileged kids. We haven't even managed to discover where Carl lives!"

"Don't give up on it yet, Ed. No one is too clever not to have left something to find however innocent it might appear to be on the surface. Let's take a look at Avant Vehicles, they're bound to have a website?"

"We've come this far, but I don't know what you expect to find. You take a look while I find us some coffee."

*****

"Come and take a look at this, Ed?"

We were looking at the homepage of Avant Executive Vehicles which showed four men and a woman posing for the camera surrounded by a number of very expensive cars. A Rolls Royce, a Bentley, a Porsche, a Lamborghini and a vehicle I instantly recognised as the Mercedes ML 65 AMG that Pip had done a fine job of trashing.

"That Merc. Unlike all the other cars, it's got a personalised number plate. I'm going back in to the DVLA and find out if it's either owned by Avant or registered to an individual."

Ten minutes later and eureka!

"Carl Stephen Matterson. Address is Folly House, The Bishops Avenue, Hampstead, London N2. I think I've heard about that road."

"Google it then."

Donny's hands flew over the keyboard then whistling through his teeth, showed me his search results. "It says here that The Bishops Avenue is the most expensive address outside of Mayfair, Belgravia or Grosvenor Square with property prices regularly fetching in excess of thirty million pounds.

Now, listen to this. One such property was sold to its current owner in 2014 for a staggering thirty-eight million. Folly House, situated overlooking Hampstead Heath boasts ten bedrooms, all of which are en-suite, seven reception rooms, one indoor and one outdoor swimming pool, tennis courts and a helipad, all set in six acres of formal gardens.

I think we can safely say that our Carl hit the big time if he can afford a pad like that!"

Chapter Twenty.

"T *hirty-eight million? No house is worth thirty-eight mill!"*

"Maybe, maybe not, but it does explain how he's able to throw money around like so much confetti."

"Pip, Callum and I pretty much wrecked his 'copter, and made it so that Merc four-by-four on the website would need a total rebuild. He was more concerned about his wife's reaction to having her brand-new car wrecked, than the money."

"Surely he can't have made all his money by prostituting kids?"

"I told you, Callum recognised his voice on that phone message. He's into drugs on an industrial scale, and probably that company in Equatorial wherever is where he keeps it. We'll never know for certain.

Let's sleep on it and see if we come up with anything else come the morning. If not, I'm going to find me a straight copper and tell him what we know."

*****

"Could I speak to Inspector Tony Bushby please? My name is Edward Anderson."

"Hold the line, Mr Anderson, and I'll see if he's in his office."

Five minutes later and...... "Inspector Bushby. How may I help you?"

"Hello Inspector. You might not remember me but my name is Edward Anderson. We met in St. Stephens Square last Christmas where I gave you a Bank Debit card and a mobile phone."

"I remember. What is it I can help you with, son?"

"I have information for you, very sensitive information."

"About what, may I ask?"

"I can't tell you that. I need proof-positive you're on the level first."

"I see. What do I have to do in order to gain your trust?"

"Not much. I know how much sat in the account that could be accessed by that card. I need you to prove to me that it was handed over to the right people and that it was all accounted for officially. Do that and I'll give you information that might give you both the person who made that threat to Vincent, plus a whole lot more."

"You must be very frightened about something."

"I am. If you're not on the up and up and the person I'm frightened of gets wind of what I need to tell you, then without meaning to sound over-melodramatic, you'll be looking at my dead body together with quite a few others. Take me seriously. I'm not joking."

"Are you happy enough to come to Birmingham Central Police Station? I can show you all the proof you need right up to the signature of my Chief Constable, HM Treasury documentation where the moneys were lodged pending further investigation."

"Good enough. What day and at what time?"

"Whenever is convenient for you."

"Give me an hour?"

"I'll be here."

*****

"So, let me show you evidence that I'm honest Tony, a career cop and not one who's on the take. This file should give you all the proof you need so read it and take your time."

I flicked through reams of documents, saw the exact amount which I knew that had been on the account, all signed off to the Treasury by the Chief Constable and witnessed by a high-ranking Treasury official.

"I'm satisfied and I'm sorry for being cautious, but once I explain things to you, I know you'll understand why."

It took me over an hour to tell him everything we knew, from Callum's participation with the parties, how he recognised the voice on the phone message, out trips to the house, collecting the kids and our taking Donny to safety. I also told him about the snuff arranged for Callum and his subsequent decision to seek sanctuary in London together with all the information we'd unearthed.

Inspector Bushby put his head in his hands.

"This goes beyond my remit, Edward. I have to pass this upstairs."

"Look, Mr Bushby. We're all shitting ourselves. I'm scared of my own shadow and can't trust anyone except you. How can I be sure whoever you pass this on to isn't in cahoots with this Carl animal? He organised a snuff for Callum. He'd watch a young boy get murdered just for money, someone that wouldn't hurt a fly, but then we come along with the beginnings of a case that could take him down for life. He wouldn't think twice about killing the lot of us. Not just Pip, Donny and myself, but all the boys that took part in those parties. He'd go to any lengths to cover his tracks, so you better make bloody sure that whoever you tell is kosher 'cos our lives are now your direct responsibility."

He nodded his understanding then lifted the phone.

"Chief Constables office? This is Detective Inspector Bushby, and what I have to talk to him about is of the utmost urgency, not to mention highly confidential."

It took a few minutes before he was connected, and although I could only hear one side of the conversation, Mr Bushby was bullish and wasn't going to be cowed down by his boss.

"Chief Constable? My apologies for calling you directly, but certain matters have come to my attention that made it necessary....... No. Given the seriousness of this information, I don't feel comfortable going to my Chief Superintendent, the risks are too enormous, it has to be you, Sir...... All I'm able to say over the phone, is that it involves child prostitution and rape, possibly murder, a drug cartel, money laundering and there may well be more...... Thank you Sir. I'll see you in fifteen minutes."

After he put the phone down, Mr Bushby looked at me. "I've just committed a cardinal sin, Edward. Going over the head of my Chief Super would under most circumstances, get me pensioned out of the service so fast it would make your head spin, so I hope to God your telling me the truth."

"I swear. I would've brought everything with me, even Pip and Donny, but I had to be 100% sure about you first. You can have everything we've managed to uncover, we'll happily sign statements to confirm everything. Trust me, I'm not lying to you. We know what we know, but proving anything has to be down to you."

"Right then. Let us go into the holy of holy's."

Another hour to go through everything, but this time with the Chief Constable. He listened patiently and every now and again he'd ask questions. Once I'd finished, he stood up and walked to the window and looked out over the city.

"I probably shouldn't tell you this, young man, but Carl Matterson is someone who's been on our radar before. I can't tell you the whys and wherefores, but it came to nothing. He's very astute, and on occasions we thought we might be able to bring charges against him but then the trail went cold.

We will need to see everything you have and we will need statements from all of you, including this boy Callum. Are you in contact with him?"

"I can get in touch but he doesn't trust uniforms, so whether or not he'll agree to talk to you is debateable."

"Try to persuade him. Tell him that if we're successful, he can live his life without looking over his shoulder ever again. Do your finest on him. We're not interested in anything he might have done in the past, this transcends everything.

When can we expect to have this information and when are you willing to write your statements?"

"Tomorrow if that suits you. Callum might take longer to get onside."

"Good. Thank you."

He turned to Mr Bushby.

"What are you working on at the moment, Inspector?"

"Run of the mill stuff, Sir. Nothing I can't hand over to a junior officer."

"Then I'm seconding you to this office. Any dealings with these boys will be your direct responsibility, then depending on what we have, it might be necessary to set up a task force of which you will be a member. All officers chosen to work on this case must be fully vetted by you. Anyone with even the slightest connection to Matterson will be sidestepped. I want the best of the best working on this. I'll talk to the Serious Crime Squad Chief Super once we've finished here." Then looking at me, "Do you need a lift home, son?"

"No thanks. I'm good."

"Then make arrangements with Inspector Bushby and let's get this rolling."

*****

As soon as I was safely back in Digbeth, I got Pip and Donny together. We took mugs of coffee onto the wharf where we found somewhere to sit.

"How did it go?"

"Mr Bushby is straight down the line and I trust him. We then had an interview with his Chief Constable who I also think is on the level. He signed over the bank account to the Treasury people; that's as much as I could do to verify stuff. The thing is, he wants us to give statements. I knew he'd ask, but I never followed that through and Donny might be a problem."

Donny shrugged his shoulders. "You mean I might get put into care, right?"

"Well, given your age and how and where we live? I would say it's a distinct possibility."

"If that's what it takes, I'm willing to do it. I want to make sure that Carl or his weird friends won't be able to touch any kid ever again."

"It hasn't come to that yet, so hold your horses. Pip? What are your thoughts?"

"No-brainer. We go with it, Ed."

"Thank you. I mean it. Thanks very much, but it still leaves the problem of how on earth we get Callum onside."

"I think you can safely leave that to me. He um…… owes me a few favours, let's just say. He'll play ball once I point out his options, and no, don't ask what those are 'cos they go back to since before you came on the scene."

"I don't wanna know. Just get him here pronto."

*****

A very pissed off Callum, together with Donny, Pip and myself, walked the towpath into the city centre. Two days had passed since that meeting with the Chief Constable and at least the last three of us on that list needed to kick-start this investigation. Callum had a different take on things though.

"You are seriously suicidal! We're fucking dead here, you do know that? Carl isn't known for his gentle side here? He'll take us out as soon as he realises someone's onto him!"

"Time bomb waiting to blow all of us to fuck. Ed and I have left too many tracks, he was bound to catch on sooner or later what with Donny disappearing. I had a mate of mine sniffing around Stafford, the word on the street is that the place is crawling with Carl's heavies, they're turning every nook and cranny upside-down, threatening and interrogating every street kid they can find. Callum, my man? It's only a matter of time before they do the maths?"

"What do you mean?"

"They're systematically ripping Stafford apart, questioning every street kid they can find in an attempt to find out where Donny's taken himself off to. Not that I think it'll happen, but it would only take one of those lads to buckle under pressure and let on about what actually happened, and Ed and I are directly in the line of fire.

The most likely outcome is that once they realise that despite all their efforts Donny can't be found, they'll expand their search to Wolverhampton where there are kids that do know something other than rumour and speculation. Again, they'll hopefully keep their mouths well and truly shut leaving the only constant in all this being us, and we'd be a piece of piss to find."

"How would we? We've managed to keep a low profile up 'til now, so what's changed?"

"Nothing's changed, and that's our problem. If he is halfway suspicious of our involvement, he won't go harassing every kid on the streets, there's too many of them and spread over too wide an area. No, I reckon he'd target people who don't give a shit.

Where do all the dossers, alcoholics and druggies hang out? Farmers Bridge locks, that's where I kick off my investigation. We use that shortcut just about every day, we're known by those pathetic people, so it would only take a few bribes, free drugs, cash enough to stay pissed for a month, and they'll have all the information they need, if not leading them to our doorstep, but close enough to make life very risky if we stuck around."

"Very well. I'll give a statement, but then it's back to London for me."

*****

The next morning found us handing over memory sticks containing all the information we'd managed to unearth. We gave our statements to Mr Bushby, mine was fairly straight-forward, whereas Donny's and Callum's took ages to do.

Donny talked to him about the possibility of being taken into care, but Mr Bushby told him that given the Social Services would have to inform his father, and as he hadn't so far been charged with any offence that would bar him access to his son, it was too dangerous as the address of his care home would become public knowledge thus exposing Donny to a frightening degree of unacceptable risk. No, he would sit tight with us unless something happened that made that impossible.

A month on and with no news from Wolverhampton, we began to relax, but some of our boys were starting to feel the strain and that resulted in about half of them giving themselves up to the care system. Summer was coming and with warmer weather, most of those that remained took themselves off and disappeared into the city leaving just five of us to man the fort, Donny, Pip, Buba, Ian and myself.

The place felt empty once they'd left, but the upside was that we didn't need to count heads each time one of them came and went.

Amazingly, Callum kept in close contact. London was starting to lose its appeal, and while he had found a steady boyfriend, he wanted to come back to Birmingham once, and all assuming the police managed to bring a successful prosecution that would see Carl safely locked away.

Time dragged. Pip and I had managed to get up and running, not just the workshop engine, but the boat was also looking good. We had managed to find two retired engineers that were capable of restoring the machinery upstairs which helped the boredom, but then three months in, we had some positive news which Mr Bushby explained to us over a mug of coffee.

"At first the powers that be, ergo the Chief Superintendent (Serious Crime Squad) thought about tackling this child prostitution head on. We have enough evidence to charge Donny's father, enough evidence to bring minor charges against Matterson, but what we most need is access to Wootton Park so we could carry out a search for DNA then we could marry them up samples found against those you believe were involved. The problem with that is it would alert Matterson to our interest in him, and given he's a slippery creature, he would probably skip abroad to where we think he keeps his fortune. Equatorial New Guinea, and the UK Government don't have an extradition treaty, so if that's where he ended up, we would be powerless to get him back. So, given the possibility we'd lose him, we looked at the drug angle.

As you know, we can't get access to his off-shore accounts, but what we could do is alert all the major clearing banks in

Europe and ask them to report on any significant movement of funds from those accounts.

We got lucky. I guess he thought he was being clever. He tried to make a substantial payment to an account in South America by channelling it through a Swiss bank.

The thing is, this might've worked until a year or so ago. The Swiss had always been very secretive about their banking practices and clients, but because of their strong ties to the EU, they had to change tack. This bank brought this transaction to our attention, and with help from the authorities in South America, we were able to discover who the money was going to. Six weeks later, one of Matterson's many companies chartered a luxury yacht. We monitored said yacht's movements, radio transmissions and so on, and it became obvious that it was on a drug collection run. As soon as it crossed into UK waters, Customs, HMRC and Drug Squad officers boarded her and found two things of significance. In the hold, they found uncut cocaine with a street value of over twenty million pounds, but in the stateroom, the biggest prize of all. Carl Stephen Matterson complete with his pet, a ten-year-old boy, a naked ten-year-old boy, a severely traumatised naked ten-year-old boy.

Now, due to the sensitive nature of our investigation, a blanket ban was put into place that prevented the press both here and abroad from reporting this incident. Matterson appeared at a closed session at Southampton Magistrates Court and is currently in custody awaiting an appearance at the Old Baily which is scheduled for next month. His wife and four of his operatives were also charged with various offences and they too are in custody.

The youngster I told you about was assessed both for his physical condition, and also with regard to his mental state. The medics are of the opinion that he's been subjected to rape and other awful sex acts over a number of years. He will recover physically, but how well he will do mentally is in the lap of the Gods together with the best doctors and health practitioners we can find.

We've managed to get our foot in the door but there's a way still to go, and here's where you come in.

We need access to Wootton Park. You know your way around the house. You know the alarm code so it would be very helpful if you could meet us there tomorrow morning a seven o'clock."

"We'll be there, but can I ask you something? Are we out of danger?"

"Hard to say for certain, Edward. You're definitely safer than you were forty-eight hours ago. He and his wife and colleagues are housed in separate prisons and all of them are in solitary confinement, but remember how worried you were about talking to me in case I was a bent cop? Well, unfortunately there are also bent prison officers so there's always a slim chance he might bribe one to get him a mobile phone. His cell is searched regularly, but nothing in life is guaranteed. Just keep a weather eye open until we've secured a conviction. Once we have that, I think he'll realise that it's only a matter of time before we have enough evidence to put him away for the rest of his natural life. No parole boards, no arguments."

"Good enough. It'll be nice not having to stay in the shadows. How's he going to plead?"

"Not guilty of course, although with so much evidence stacked up against him, nothing short of a point of law will get him off. We'll be taking every precaution, we'll have solicitors and barristers crawling all over this case to make sure it's as watertight as possible.

Assuming he goes down, what are you plans for the future?"

Buba place his coffee on the table. "Ronny wants to put me through catering college. He reckons I could make a fine chef one day."

"And you Ian. Going to take up boxing?"

Ian laughed. "Actually, while I know I look intimidating, I have a soft centre. If I was young enough to go back to school, then I would, but instead I'll go to college and with luck, qualify as a teacher."

"Pip?"

"Take my heavy goods licence. I love driving, it's all I've ever wanted to do."

"Donny?"

"Definitely go back to school. Ed wants to go back to Solihull and get his place smartened up. We'll live there and with a bit of luck I can get a scholarship to Hatton Grammar, finish my education then see what happens."

"And you, Edward. Got any plans of your own?"

"Similar. Finish my education, then I want to open this dump up as a Heritage Museum, run it as a charity for those kids living on the streets."

"Then I sincerely hope it happens for all of you. I better get away now before I get my arse chewed. I'll see you in the morning."

Chapter Twenty-One.

I t was with a feeling of enormous relief as we went about our daily lives knowing that Carl and his thugs were soon to stand trial. Another reason, was knowing that the bust that had brought him to court didn't involve us so there was the possibility he wouldn't suspect our involvement and perhaps the heat had died down. None the less, we were cautious when we went out.

We had met a team of forensic scientists, Mr Bushby and some other officers at Wootton Park as arranged, showed them around, and following the tour they promptly sealed off all the bedrooms, concentrating their efforts on the playroom. I told them about my poisoning incident, so after a cursory examination of the floors, work surfaces and play areas that confirmed someone had tried to do a clean-up job, went for the places that might still reveal something of interest. Following that, we left for my house in Solihull where I half expected it to have been turned over by Carl's people, but it was as we had left it.

I followed the Old Baily's website and discovered that he was due to appear on September 12th in Court number one, and come the time we all followed the case as reported in the press, telly we didn't have.

His legal team had cross-examined all the witnesses rigorously, argued obscure points of law, but never once did they deny the charges outright. They tried to argue that the yacht had been boarded outside of UK territorial waters thus making it sound like an act of piracy, but the coastguard cutter that had escorted the boarding party had an electronic log which disproved their argument, and actually, it made them look stupid.

The young boy didn't appear in person, his evidence was given over a video link with his face hidden from the camera, but that didn't stop him from being on the sharp end of some pretty aggressive cross-examination, however the presiding Judge soon put a stop to that.

It was also reported that at no time did any of the defendants show any remorse, and sick fuck that Carl is, apparently, he was smiling during the boy's evidence, but finally the jury was sent away so they could come to a verdict.

On three consecutive days, they reported that they still hadn't come to a decision, then on day four they announced their findings.

Carl came top of the list.

Charge one. Being in possession of class A drugs, to wit, two hundred kilograms of uncut cocaine, Guilty by a unanimous verdict.

Charge two. Attempting to import class A drugs. Ditto the amount, and ditto the verdict.

Charge three. Abduction and false imprisonment of a minor. Guilty by a unanimous verdict.

Charge four. Six counts of Statutory rape. Guilty by a unanimous verdict.

Charge five. Fifteen counts of Committing an act of gross indecency. Guilty by a unanimous verdict.

Charge six. Ten counts of Assault occasioning Grievous bodily harm with intent. Guilty by a unanimous verdict.

His wife.

Charge one. Aiding and abetting the importation of class A drugs. Guilty by a majority verdict.

Charge two. Knowingly assisting in the abduction and false imprisonment of a minor. Guilty by a majority verdict.

Charge three. Six counts of Perverting the course of justice. Guilty by a unanimous verdict.

Then came the four thugs, each of whom had been charged with the same offences, although the verdicts reached were read to the court individually. However, the end result was the same for each of them.

Charge one. Aiding and abetting the importation of class A drugs. Guilty by a majority verdict.

Charge two. Procurement of a child for the purposes of sex. Guilty by a unanimous verdict.

Charge three. Knowingly assisting in the abduction and false imprisonment of a minor. Guilty by a unanimous verdict.

Charge four. Six counts of Perverting the course of justice. Guilty by a unanimous verdict.

By the end of the day, all six of them had been found guilty of all charges brought against them but the Judge deferred sentence for two weeks, remanding them in custody for the duration.

I called Callum.

"Yeah. I've already heard! I wanna come back to Brum, that is if you'll take me in?"

"It's still your place and it would be great having you back."

"Can I um…… bring my boyfriend?"

"Of course? I don't want a miserable Callum cluttering up the place!"

"You'll like him. He's another egghead just like you!"

"There's a lot of us around what with Donny wanting to get back to school, Buba going to catering college, Ian want to train to be a teacher and Pip taking his HGV licence. You'll be the only numbskull on the premises!"

"Fuck you, Anderson. I used to like you!"

"Still got a silver tongue I see."

"Nothing much changes, Ed. I wouldn't want to be a disappointment to you."

"You could never disappoint me.

What are you planning on doing once you're back?"

"Dunno. I'll think of summat."

"How's about doing an RYA Helmsman course? We have that sodding great big boat and it would be good to have someone who can drive the damn thing? I want to set stuff in motion so we can open up this hovel as a working museum. The boat was built here, so why not deck it out and do cruises."

"Could do I suppose. Sounds like fun!

I better scoot now, but I'll give you a call once I've got everything squared away at this end. I wanna be back to hear the sentencing 'cos that will signal party time. A real party. Round up the boys and have a blast."

*****

The day sentences were handed down found us back in Solihull where we could catch up on the news as soon as it broke.

Carl received a thrashing from the Judge telling him he posed a real danger to society. A paedophile drug baron who had shown no remorse during the entire trial. He was handed the maximum penalty for drug importation, a fifteen-year period behind bars with no possibility of parole until he'd served at least twelve years.

For possession, he received eight years, abduction and false imprisonment, a further eight years, Statutory rape he got hammered with a life term. Minimum time before parole would be considered, twenty years, counts of ABH with intent, ten years and for the counts of gross indecency, a further ten years giving a total sentence of sixty-eight years, but these to be served concurrently, meaning he could be out after serving just a twenty-year term.

His wife got off with lighter sentences.

Aiding and abetting importation, five years, Assisting the abduction and false imprisonment of a minor got her clouted with seven years, but the longest sentence was for Perverting the course of justice for which the judge handed down a fifteen-year term, with no possibility of parole until she had served at least ten.

The four thugs received the same treatment, and all things considered, we were happy enough with the outcome.

I had a call from Mr Bushby.

"Are you all happy with the sentences?"

"By and Large. Shame those will be served concurrently rather than consecutively."

"I know what you mean, but the justice system has to be seen to be fair. If His Lordship had swung the axe harder, then an appeal of sentence would be inevitable and something that would be a waste of public money.

Think on the positive. If we can nail him for all the other stuff, the likely outcome will be that he'll never see the outside world again. Life will mean life, Edward, and he won't be released unless he's at death's door. There's a hearing next month that will see him stripped of his assets. We aren't in a position to touch his offshore interests, but everything else he'll lose and if he makes any attempt to transfer assets from abroad, we'll take them as well.

On a lighter note, there will be a substantial reward coming to all of you, plus Donny and Callum will receive a pay-out from the Criminal Injury Compensation Board.

I can't tell you anything about our ongoing investigations other than they're starting to look very promising, but just remember. These are highly complex, and it may well take years before we're ready to go to court. Stay happy, and if possible, keep the little-un's out of mischief!"

*****

Back at Bishops Wharf we broke the good news to the lads who were in the loop, which somehow turned out to be all of them.

Two days on and we met with the boys from Wolverhampton who told us that now that they didn't feel the need to stay undercover, would co-operate with the police and give statements. Also, they would have a quiet chat to some of the other boys involved to see if they could persuade them on board. They thought that most would, but some were still very traumatised and might take some time to talk around.

I called Mr Bushby.

"I know you're not allowed to tell me what's happening or what progress you've made, but we've talked to couple of boys from Wolverhampton who were involved in those gigs at Wotton Park. They're prepared to give you statements, plus they'll talk to the other boys they know. Would that help you?"

"You're right. I can't tell you anything. You are material witnesses and it would render your evidence inadmissible in court. If his legal team came close to suspecting we'd talked to you off the record, our case might be dismissed on a technicality, but having said that, we would be very interested in gathering as much information as possible. If those boys are willing to come forward then fine, we'd like to hear what they have to say."

"We were thinking of getting everyone together at our place; not so you could take statements, but some of them are terrified and might need to hear from you about how they might be treated."

"That might work. Do you feel comfortable with us coming to you?"

"Perfectly comfortable, but don't expect a palace."

"You've talked to your clan then?"

"Callum, Pip and Donny. If we do it on a Saturday afternoon, the rest of our lot will be out and about. Some of the boys from Wolverhampton are still in school so it might be the best time for them as well."

"See what you can organise then call me. You know how they'll be treated. With sympathy and respect. We're not concerned about any past misdemeanours or petty crimes they might've committed, we could even offer them immunity from prosecution. All we're interested in, Edward, is getting sufficient evidence together to file solid charges against some very evil and dangerous individuals."

"Thanks Mr Bushby. I'll call you once I have news."

*****

"Ed? This is Scott from Wolverhampton. Got a few minutes to talk?"

"Yeah, no worries. What's the news?"

"As you already know, Rich and me are willing to hook up with the police, plus I managed to get a few more on-side but not all of them. Problem is, they're still scared half out of their minds, not only 'bout what might happen if Carl suspects anything and manages to put something together from his prison cell, but they're all shitting themselves about talking to the law and I dunno how best to deal with it."

"Yes, I was frightened that might be the case, but I've talked to our man and he's happy to meet anyone who comes along. Honestly, Scott, they've nothing to be worried about, and if you could see that for yourself then you could use your own experiences to convince those who don't want to get involved."

"Okay. When and where?"

"Saturday next at our place. Get the Metro to Moor Street station, call us once you're near and we'll come and meet you. Make it for around two in the afternoon."

"We'll be there. Bye, Ed."

*****

Mr Bushby was very gentle in his approach and managed to settle the boy's nerves from the word go. He explained the history about how I'd first contacted him; not the precise details as he explained he was still working to bring further charges of drug distribution and possible murder against someone who I had been the provider of information. I guessed he was talking about the charge card and Vincent's disappearance as he nodded in my direction.

He then went on to tell them about the hoops I had him jump through to prove he wasn't on the take and that he could be trusted, then finished with a plea to them to mirror my trust so he could put Carl and others away for ever.

Callum chipped in with his own verification.

"Look, guys? Most of you know me, and remember me as the last person who would have any dealings with the fuzz, but even I trust Mr Bushby. So, the bottom line? If I can do it then so can you lot. Come on, let's help the guy!"

There were questions which Mr Bushby answered candidly and honestly. He didn't tell them that it was going to be a walkover, in fact he said that it was going to be a tough job to pull everything together; tough but possible, but only if they were prepared to help.

One of the younger boys mentioned that he thought that his father might be involved, and asked if he would he be prosecuted.

"Depending on what we uncover, then he might well be, son. It's hard to say without your evidence and what else we might find out about him. Does that worry you?"

"Yeah. He's a bastard, but he's still my dad."

"We can't pick and choose, son. If he's been up to no good then he has to face the consequences of his actions. I can't change, nor would I change my answer just to make you feel good. Honesty, remember?"

"It's okay. I'll still tell you everything."

And so it went on until the meeting broke up and we saw Mr Bushby off the premises. Useful and productive I think it's called.

*****

Weeks turned to months, fifteen to be precise, then one day Donny and I were working in the garden back in Solihull when Marie, Pip's girlfriend called us into the house.

"I thought you might like to see what they're reporting on in the lunchtime news. Something to do with a paedophile ring and people being taken in for questioning."

We slipped out of our shoes to save getting dirt on the new carpets and sat down in front of the TV where Pip, Callum and his boyfriend joined us having been decorating the stairwell.

The Anchor-man handed over to a reporter.

"Thank you, Charlie. The police are being rather tight-lipped about this morning's events; however they have told us that following months of investigations, they raided homes and business premises across the country and made a number of arrests which they say are in related to a suspected child prostitution ring. Forensic teams have removed what we believe to be computer equipment and personal items and are also carrying out detailed examinations of these properties.

In addition, four premises in France, three in Germany and two in the Netherlands have also been raided in a co-ordinated operation they call Operation Echo.

The European Crime Agency together with the Home Office here in the UK, have banned us from reporting further details, an injunction which, naturally, we will honour.

Peter Swan, BBC News, outside Birmingham City Police Headquarters."

The shot went back to the studio and the Anchor-man.

"As Peter told us there, we are unable to talk about the names of those who have been arrested nor can we report on locations, however most of these raids took place in and around the West Midlands then with one in Hampstead, three in Yorkshire and one in Manchester. Many of those taken into custody are prominent members of society including politicians, high ranking military officers, solicitors and barristers together with prominent names from industry. We have little information regarding the raids in Europe, but we're working closely with our colleagues in those countries and will report what we can, when we can.

We have requested interviews with the Commander of the Regional Serious Crime Squad in the West Midlands together with the Chief Constable, however our request was refused but issued a statement which reads;

"Whilst we recognise that the public has a right to be kept informed, sensitive investigations are still on-going and this has to take precedence over everything. We look to the media for their support and co-operation, and members of the public for their understanding."

"In other headlines today......."

We switched the TV to standby.

Callum was the first to speak.

"You reckon......?"

"Has to be. For me, Hampstead was the dead give-away as that's where Carl lived."

"Yeah, but, Ed? He's already in choky, so why go back there now?"

"Big place. Maybe they feel they missed something."

"Probably. I mean, if there was something else going down apart from Carl's stuff, I think I might have got a whiff of it but there was nothing. Just your normal pervy punters on the street."

"Don't tell me you went back on the rent when you were in London?"

"Nope, but when you've had those experiences in the past, you kinda pick up on the vibes and I picked up on Jack Shit. There were the boys out on the street plying their trade as there are in most big cities, but I never caught up with anything like what went down here."

Just then my phone squawked at me, and noticing it was a withheld number, promptly ignored it, but then moments later, voice mail.

I dialled into it and listened.

"Edward? This is Inspector Bushby. Obviously you don't like answering calls from blocked numbers, I don't either, but could you call me on the number you used before as I need to talk to all of you. Thanks."

I put the phone to one side and looked at the others. "That was Mr Bushby. Maybe we're going to get some news at last."

*****

Later that same afternoon we sat around as Mr Bushby set out his stall. "I'm assuming you all caught the news about the raids carried out earlier today? Police forces across the country together with our colleagues in Europe made a total of nineteen arrests with more to follow in the coming days. We've done a phenomenal amount of work over the past year so we're confident that all these individuals were involved with the activities at Wootton Park have been arrested, and also there's evidence that this goes beyond just being a UK problem, we know that similar setups are going on in several European countries together with America, South Africa and Russia.

Now, we expect full co-operation from the authorities in each of these countries with the possible exception of Russia where we have little expectation that they'll agree to extraditions, but that said, already we've received assurances that they will carry out their own investigations, and to that end I have been asked to fly to Moscow this evening and brief them on what we already know.

The reason for telling you this is because we can see light at the end of this very long tunnel, and depending on how those we might charge plea at Magistrates Court, I'm putting you on notice that it might not be that long before you're required to give evidence.

I don't want you to worry yourselves over this, the prosecuting team will speak to you prior to that time, refresh your memories, show you your statements and guide you through your evidence.

One other point; something I'm sure they will also reiterate; stick to the facts at all times. Don't be tempted into speculating about what you *might have believed* was going on, just what you actually witnessed, what you saw and what you did. The defence will try every trick in the book in order to undermine your version of events, so no guess work please.

Those of you under the age of eighteen have an automatic right to anonymity and we'll try to get the Courts to impose injunctions on the media to prevent the remainder of you from being exposed. Not a done deal, but given the nature of these cases, I'm reasonably confident that their Lordships will look favourably on such a request.

ave any of you lads got questions?"

Donny's hand shot up. "Just the one, Sir. Has my father been arrested?"

"Yes, Donny, he has.

Now, if there's nothing else, I've got a suitcase to pack."

Chapter Twenty-Two.

Donny was quiet following Mr Bushby's visit; no doubt preoccupied with his Dad's arrest and the possibility he might have to testify at his trial. I thought about talking to him about it, but instead I just gave him a cuddle before going back out into the garden to clear up the hedge clippings, hoping that it would get the message across that I understood how he must be feeling.

*****

The house and surrounding gardens were starting to look like a family home again. We had made a start on the ground floor by completely redecorating the kitchen then followed up by the dining room, lounge and hallway. We ripped up all the carpets and ordered new replacements; neutral colours of a light grey fleck which lightened the rooms but would also be forgiving if someone forgot to remove their outside shoes.

The stairwell and landing had proved to be the hardest task as they'd been papered and stripping the walls had been a bitch, mainly due to the high walls and the discovery that none of us were keen on heights. The downstairs toilet was going to be gutted. The hand basin was cracked and no amount of cleaning would shift the stains around the toilet bowl. We had chosen their replacements but they were on back order, so another job for another time.

There were going to be six of us living there once the redecoration had been completed. Callum and Mark, (Callum's boyfriend), Pip and Marie and Donny and me. That left us with two bedrooms out of the five, one of which we might utilise as a sort of office-come-study room as at least three of us would be going back into the education system, leaving Pip to concentrate of his HGV training with Callum and Mark to do the two RYA courses so we could operate the boat in conjunction with our museum idea.

We had talked to the head instructor at the Royal Yachting Association, and his idea of Callum and Mark doing two courses each made a lot of sense. Their training boat was a modern fifty-five-footer whereas ours was a vintage seventy-footer. Get to grips with the shorter modern boat, then spend two weeks getting comfortable with the larger older one during which time they would receive one-on-one tuition.

Mark was a total contrast to Callum. He was younger by two-and-a-half years, softly spoken and well mannered. Set this against Callum's gobby, up-front attitude and complete lack of decorum made them absolute opposites. They were devoted to each other despite their differences, and it was good to see their enthusiasm for the boat thing. Pip thinks they will end up being Boat Bores, but who cares so long as they're happy.

All of us like Marie. Not only is she very pretty, she has a sense of humour that would lift our spirits when we felt low. She told us that she dropped out of school aged sixteen, but for all that, she was very intelligent and helped me massively when it came to teaching our younger kids.

Donny is lovely and I'm totally smitten with him! We share the same bed, we cuddle and kiss; sometimes things get a bit touchy-feely, but nothing heavy had gone on between us. This was mostly due to the possibility we'd have to give evidence in court, and this way, if under cross-examination, questions were asked about our relationship, we could be 100% truthful and say that our relationship was purely platonic.

I hoped that would change!

*****

It was two months before we heard anything regarding going to court. We'd caught up with some of the Wolverhampton lads appearing, and by all accounts had received a grilling from the defence lawyers during cross-examination. All the men standing trial were eventually found guilty and received substantial custodial sentences which made us feel better about our own outcomes.

Poor Donny had two summonses to answer, the first of which was concerning his father.

In the event, he entered a plea of guilty meaning Donny didn't appear in court, but the guy who had raped him repeatedly was a different matter altogether.

This guy was looking for a fight.

Donny, being now sixteen, was asked if he was willing to stand up in court to give his evidence or would he rather appear by video link with his face hidden from view.

Plucky sod that he is, went for an appearance but treated nicely he most definitely wasn't.

They tried to argue that Donny had fabricated his evidence in order to destroy the good name and record of a distinguished member of Her Majesty's Navy; everything was a tissue of lies; a plot to subvert and undermine the defence of the realm. Claim and counterclaim, accusations and arguments until the judge slapped them down by asking the defence council to submit evidence to the court in order to substantiate their allegations or else shut the fuck up, or words to that effect. (That, by the way, and in case you hadn't already guessed, was Callum's version of events!)

Anyhow, he got sent down for eighteen years. Donny reckoned he'd have popped his clogs well before he would be eligible for parole.

From there on, they dropped like flies with only a few putting up a feeble defence. But then came the big one.

Carl was brought to court.

He was facing multiple charges of child prostitution, rape, making and distributing indecent images of children, murder of three young boys, and surprise, surprise, the murder of one Vincent Sean Connor.

Carl looked old. His features were sagging, as I guessed was his fighting spirit. He had pleaded Not Guilty at the Magistrates hearing, but as Marie told us afterwards, hurried and intense discussions with his legal team resulted in him slumping down in the dock, then raising his hand as he changed his plea to Guilty on all charges.

He was finished.

He was sentenced to life imprisonment to serve a minimum term of forty years before parole would even be considered.

Once Carl had been taken down, the judge took the unusual step of addressing the press gallery. This summing up was widely reported on TV and newspapers across the world.

"I wish to pay tribute to those who brought these horrific events to the notice of the police.

These people who I refer to were only children at that time, and not only that, but all of them were underprivileged and homeless, most certainly not used to willingly talk with the authorities, so the courage they found within themselves to come forward should be recognised by society as a whole.

We, all of us should be reminded of the goodness and virtue to be found in even the forgotten and neglected in our world, and to this end, I intend to meet these courageous young people and extend not only my own personal thanks, but also on behalf of all children who are now able to walk the streets safe in the knowledge that evil and dangerous people who would otherwise harm them, are now behind bars.

Ladies and gentlemen? This court is adjourned. Thank you."

*****

Back at the house I suddenly felt very tired. Since Callum told Pip and I about what had happened to him and the parties at Wootton Park, I think I'd been living on pure adrenaline, but the adrenaline rush had disappeared and the feeling of anti-climax brought tears to my eyes.

I can't remember the last time I had a good cry; I had become hardened to life on the streets, conditioned to the hardships and being seen as socially unacceptable, but now my life was crashing in on top of me.

I took myself off to bed leaving the other guys celebrating downstairs. I tried to cry, I mean, I really did, but nothing came, I just lay face up staring at the ceiling.

I've turned into a heartless bastard. What on earth happened to that boy who used to care about others? Where's all that compassion gone? Damn it, I can't even cry anymore!'

*****

think I must have drifted off to sleep, because the next thing I was aware of was Donny running his fingers through my hair.

"How are you feeling, Ed?"

"Miserable. My head is telling me we did a good thing, but my heart is telling me something completely different."

"How so?"

"How many people have appeared in court aside from Carl who I don't give a toss about?"

"Nineteen, and more to come according to Mr Bushby who you've just missed. Why do you ask?"

"More?"

"They're still working on stuff. It won't involve any of us though."

"That's nineteen people whose lives we've trashed. Nineteen-plus families, torn to shreds, their children, unable to hold their heads high even though they're innocent of any wrong-doing."

"Would you rather have those men walking the streets; free to molest, rape and murder innocent kids?

Somewhere in a lime pit on a farm, innocent kids slowly decomposed leaving no trace they even existed, not even their

288

DNA; having been tortured, raped and murdered. Who's mourning their loss? Who's crying over them? Nobody! They don't even have names! They don't even have identities…… but we know they're there!"

"I'm sorry. Joined up thinking isn't working for me at the moment."

"Yes, well. Why don't you come down stairs? Callum and Pip are organising a shindig back at Digbeth tonight. All the boys are going to be there, and maybe when you look into their eyes you will realise that they will never again be subjected to such inhumane treatment and all because you, Pip and Callum took on the might of Carls enterprise and won!"

"Let me splash some water in my face and I'll be down in a minute.

I'm so sorry, Donny. I'm a selfish arsehole."

"No, you're not. This thing has occupied your every waking moment, and now it's over there's a void in your life. Come on, Ed? We have each other, we have our work cut out just getting back into full time education, and then there's the museum to think about.

It's time to move forward now.

A time to forget what's past.

A time for us to get Another Life.

Printed in Great Britain
by Amazon